FORBIDDEN LOVE

FORBIDDEN LOVE

Catherine Vincent

Chivers Press • G.K. Hall & Co.
Bath, England   Thorndike, Maine USA

This Large Print edition is published by Chivers Press, England, and by G.K. Hall & Co., USA.

Published in 2000 in the U.K. by arrangement with the author.

Published in 2000 in the U.S. by arrangement with Juliet Burton Literary Agency.

U.K. Hardcover   ISBN 0-7540-4198-0   (Chivers Large Print)
U.K. Softcover   ISBN 0-7540-4199-9   (Camden Large Print)
U.S. Softcover   ISBN 0-7838-9098-2   (Nightingale Series Edition)

The text of this Large Print edition is unabridged.
Other aspects of the book may vary from the original edition.

Set in 16 pt. New Times Roman.

Printed in Great Britain on acid-free paper.

British Library Cataloguing in Publication Data available

Library of Congress Cataloging-in-Publication Data

    Vincent, Catherine, 1951–
      Forbidden love / Catherine Vincent.
          p. cm.—(G.K. Hall large print Nightingale series)
      ISBN 0-7838-9098-2 (lg. print : sc : alk. paper)
      1. Businesswomen—Fiction. 2. Large type books. I. Title.
    II. Series.
    PR6072.I48 F67 2000
    823'.914—dc21   00–039533

CHAPTER ONE

It was ten o'clock on a Monday morning, usually Ginny's busiest time. But today the office was so quiet she could have heard a pin drop.

'Will?' she queried, dark eyes fixed on the young man standing uneasily in front of her.

'Darling, it won't be for long,' he said, shrugging defensively, but he still didn't meet her eyes.

'Not for long?' she echoed incredulously. 'Oh, Will.'

Disbelief momentarily froze her tongue. This was Will, her Will. Surely he hadn't said what she thought he'd said. It wasn't possible. She couldn't have heard him right.

'You can't mean it?' she protested, wide-eyed.

'Oh, Ginny.' He sighed. 'I can't see any other way. It isn't my fault if things have gone wrong.'

'Not your fault!'

She couldn't believe her ears. Was this the same Will Shepherd she'd known for the last twelve months, her office manager, the man she loved? Only a few days before, he'd positively insisted on announcing the date of their wedding. Now he was saying they would have to call it off, for the time being, at least.

1

'It won't be for ever,' he repeated doggedly.

She was gripped by a moment's hatred of him. He didn't seem to have any idea of what he was asking, what it would mean to her, to both of them.

'Well, I still don't understand,' she replied flatly.

'Ginny, please.'

Ginny glanced up, her attention caught by his tone. It was harsh, sharp with misery. There was no mistaking the fear. Instantly, her heart rate leaped into overdrive, beating an uncomfortable tattoo in her breast. Darling Will, he meant everything to her. She would have forgiven him almost anything, willingly. But surely, this was too much to ask. Even for him?

'But why? What has this man, this Aleksander Bergovich, got to do with us, with our wedding?' she questioned.

'Everything,' Will said gruffly, his head bent. 'If he lets me down, I've got nothing left. No prospects, no job, even. How can we get married then?'

'Easily!' she retorted. 'I love you, not your job or your prospects. Besides,' she added swiftly, 'we can manage on my salary for a time.'

'No,' Will broke in, his mouth a stubborn line. 'I would never want that!'

She threw him a sideways glance, shaking her dark head, and he took a step forward, putting out an uncertain hand to touch her slim shoulder. Instinctively her fingers closed over his. He was usually so charming, cheerful and full of fun. With his ready smile and personable good looks, he had risen fast in the company and at the ripe old age of twenty-seven, he was made head of the firm's entire overseas sales operation.

Determined to prove himself, he had entered into a deal with a foreign competitor from one of the newly-liberated Eastern bloc countries. Success would have brought major new outlets for the firm's business software and a slice of the action for Will himself, if he'd managed to pull it off. He'd been over the moon, full of the opportunities it opened up, for the firm, for himself. He hadn't stopped talking about the wonderful life they would live. But the deal turned out to be more of a gamble than he'd imagined.

With breezy optimism, he'd committed the firm's resources up to the hilt. Then things hadn't gone quite according to plan. Ginny had no idea how it had actually happened. Will always kept the finer details to himself. All she knew for certain was that the owner of the foreign company, one Aleksander Bergovich, had become more and more difficult, refusing to sign the final contracts without further concessions which Will wasn't in a position to give. And without his signature, the whole deal would fall through.

3

'Oh, Will,' she murmured, her heart squeezing with pity for him.

Sighing, she reached up to touch his mouth, the lips thinned and anxious under her fingertips. He may have been headstrong, over-confident even, but he hadn't been driven by greed or ambition. She knew him better than that. But as for this Aleksander Bergovich, she wasn't nearly so sure about him. If even half of what Will said about him was true, the man was a truly formidable figure, formidable and highly dangerous. As head of a powerful industrial empire, his word was law, his decisions absolute. And somehow, somewhere, Will had managed to get on the wrong side of him.

'Please, Ginny,' Will murmured, his voice breaking into her thoughts, 'you must understand. How can I possibly think about getting married with all this hanging over my head? I might end up in prison.'

'Can Bergovich really do that?'

'You'd better believe it,' he insisted tightly.

'Is there nothing we can do?' she queried. 'Can't we talk to the man?'

It seemed infinitely logical to her. Bergovich had to be open to reason. He wanted to expand into the West, and their company could offer him the quickest way. The work towards it was already half done.

'I don't know.'

Will shook his head, obviously still not

entirely convinced.

'I'd rather you didn't get mixed up in any of this.'

'Rubbish,' she countered, dismissing his protests.

She was his fiancée, for heaven's sake, already mixed up in his life. How could he imagine anything else?

'Oh, Ginny, Ginny,' he said, seeing her determined face, upturned towards him, 'what could you do that I haven't tried already?'

'Probably not a lot,' Ginny conceded, though she knew that wasn't strictly true.

Will was full of ideas, always raring to go, but wasn't it her organisation, her innate attention to detail, which generally kept him on course?

'Bergovich isn't exactly the kind of man you're used to,' he persisted.

'He can't murder me,' she broke in, smiling, trying to lighten the mood.

She had never before seen Will look so lost, so beaten, and she was determined he was going to accept her help, whether he liked it or not!

'I'm your secretary,' she reminded him firmly. 'If we present a united front to this Bergovich character, maybe he'll be more inclined to listen.'

'I don't know,' he said hesitantly, smiling that sweet, lopsided smile of his she could never resist. 'I don't want you to be hurt or humiliated.'

But he was already halfway to agreement. She could see it in his shaky smile, in his eyes meeting hers for the first time that day.

'Do you really think we can?' he queried finally, a tiny thread of hope creeping into his voice.

'Will Shepherd,' she responded at once, eyebrows raised in mock-concern, 'do you really want to marry me?'

She didn't get the chance to say anymore. Instantly, his arms went about her, gathering her to him.

'Never think anything else,' he whispered, his expression anguished, 'not even in fun. Believe me, if I honestly thought meeting Bergovich would make a difference, wild horses wouldn't hold me back.'

'Then isn't it worth a try?'

Slowly, he nodded, finally giving way to her persistence.

'We can try,' he admitted, 'not that I think it will do any good.'

'We'll see,' she whispered.

Tenderly, Will bent his head, his lips claiming the soft, pink cushion of her mouth, deeply, possessively, as she melted against him.

'Virginia Eve, you are incorrigible,' he whispered, releasing her at long last. 'I'm beginning to think you're right. Bergovich won't stand a chance!'

'Not one,' she agreed, her voice soft with

love.

But for the next day or so, Ginny lived on tenterhooks, hating the uncertainty, the waiting for something to happen. When Will finally came into the office, a sheepish look on his young face, the relief was enormous. Thank goodness, she breathed, now we can get this thing over with.

'Bergovich?' she asked.

'Mm, he says he'll meet us before dinner on Friday, at his hotel.'

'Good,' she stated quickly, incisively.

There was no point in hanging back, in beating about the bush.

'He wants to get things settled,' Will went on, 'and to tell the truth, so do I. The firm's getting anxious to see some return for its investments, and I'm running out of reasons for not closing the deal.'

'I know, I know. And I'm sure we'll manage to sort something out. If we can show him he'll get more out of completing the deal than by dropping the whole thing, we might persuade him to think again. It's only commonsense.'

In spite of all her brave words, by the time Friday finally came round, Ginny's nerves were definitely beginning to fray. Left to his own devices, Will had certainly let his enthusiasm run away with him, and the whole deal was in more of a tangle than she'd imagined possible. For hours they'd gone through the papers, poring over line after line of figures, checking the small print until their eyes ached. They were burning the midnight oil, night after night, trying to sort out an acceptable package, and to make matters worse, Will developed a sudden blind faith in her ability to get him off the hook which only added to the general tension.

'Will it work?' he queried, his eyes searching hers for reassurance.

She wasn't sure, she honestly wasn't sure. She'd clawed together a deal she hoped would make Bergovich sit up and take notice, offering him discounts in all the right areas, promising deliveries in record time. It would be hard work for a time, very hard, but it was just about manageable.

'I hope so,' she said, standing on tiptoe to press her mouth on to his.

What else could she say? There was nothing left to do now but hope.

The journey home went without incident, and she parked the car in its usual place. Once inside, she made herself a coffee, taking it with her into the bathroom, slipping out of her clothes to take a shower with a mind that was carefully blank. The thought of the evening ahead didn't exactly unnerve her. Wary she might be, so much depended on this meeting, but to tell the truth, she'd be only too glad to get it over with. It had been hanging over her head for too long, interfering with her plans.

And as for Aleksander Bergovich, she

couldn't believe that all Will said about him was true. The man was keen for success in the West, wasn't he? So, surely his business sense would prevail in the end. With speculative eyes, she went to her wardrobe, searching for something suitable to wear.

'This will do,' she decided at last, lifting out a dark green trouser suit.

It was elegantly cut in a sleekly expensive gabardine, but with its fitted jacket and narrow pants, it was strictly formal. Deliberately, she teamed it with a tailored ivory shirt she only ever wore for work.

'Good.'

She nodded, her eyes resting approvingly on the cool, erect figure looking back at her from the full length mirror. The completed outfit was just right, super-efficient, business-like, the very impression she wanted to give.

The doorbell cut abruptly into her thoughts, telling her Will had arrived.

'Oh, well,' she said to her reflection, 'time to go,' and with a determined smile nailed to her lips, she collected her bag and went out to meet him.

Will was standing in the porch, waiting for her, the breeze lifting his hair. He looked so young, so boyishly handsome in his grey suit, that her heart turned over. Pulling her straight into his arms, he bent and kissed her.

'Nervous?' he queried, and she nodded.

'A bit,' she admitted.

'Me, too.'

Quickly, she took his arm, before he could start having second thoughts, and he escorted her through the gathering darkness, towards the scarlet, open-topped sports car standing at the kerb.

'Where exactly are we going?' she asked.

'To Bergovich's hotel, in Mayfair,' he replied. 'Then,' he whispered into her ear, his tone conspiratorial, 'we'll have dinner at a little Italian place I know in town, just the two of us. How about that?'

'Sounds fabulous.'

'You'll love it,' he promised.

The drive was a short one, away from the glittering lights of the West End and along the edge of Hyde Park. It was a crisp evening in late September, fine and clear but with the first touch of autumn in the air. Before long they left the busy roads behind, driving deep into the domain of the very rich. It was quieter there, the sound of the traffic muted in the wide, exclusive streets. The hotel itself, a slender, high-rise edifice of glass and mellow brick, was easy to find. Approached by a broad sweep of marble steps, an elegant awning hung over the portico, protecting its impressive splendour from any suggestion of wind or rain.

Lights blazed out from the foyer, and the wide, glass doors slid open with well-oiled ease at the doorman's touch, allowing them through. The lobby was full of people, and

Ginny paused for a moment in the doorway.

'Second thoughts?' Will enquired, feeling her hesitation.

Something in his voice made her look up, sharply, into his face. Under the artificial lights his features seemed almost grey, and she felt a deep stab of pity for him.

'Of course not,' she whispered, squeezing his hand.

For a moment or two, Will left her, moving over to speak to the receptionist. He seemed to be chatting a lot, smiling and nodding to the girl behind the desk, and a smile tugged at Ginny's lips. Dear Will. He had to make an impression. He always did, with any woman he met. It was second nature to him. But when he turned, smiling towards her across the crowded floor, he had eyes for no-one else. Serenely, she smiled back. She knew he loved her. She had no need to worry.

'You look lovely,' he whispered as soon as he got within earshot.

'Do I need to?' she returned, raising a brow.

She thought this meeting was purely business.

'Well, it won't hurt to charm Bergovich a little.'

'I'm not here to charm him.'

Decisively, she shook her head. That wasn't the idea at all. She was here as Will's secretary, to help him put forward a business deal, not to flutter her eyelashes. If that was the kind of help he wanted, he could think again.

'Well, at least Bergovich can't eat us,' Will conceded, shrugging.

'No?' she queried.

From what he'd said about the man, Bergovich would quite happily make a meal of them both.

'Haven't you heard of eating people for breakfast?' she said, grinning.

'Well, we're safe for the moment,' he replied. 'It's still only dinner time.'

A row of lifts stood nearby, silent and waiting. Without a word, they stepped inside one, staring ahead as it rose, carrying them effortlessly towards the top floor. Ginny's mouth was dry, her mind an obstinate blank. The enormity of what they were doing had suddenly taken her breath away.

This isn't true, it can't really be happening, she thought in growing dismay. Any minute now, Will would laugh out loud and whisk her off to dinner, telling her it was all a joke. Expectantly, she looked his way, but he only squeezed her arm, doing his best to look reassuring.

'We'll be all right,' he whispered. 'Bergovich isn't a fool. He's bound to be open to reason.'

With a gloomy smile, she nodded back. What more could she say? Hadn't she told him as much herself?

They stepped out of the lift together, on to a carpet of soft grey, so thick Ginny felt she sank up to her ankles in it. Directly in front of them stood the door to the penthouse suite.

'Go on,' Ginny urged, and Will gave a tentative knock on its surface.

Almost at once, it was flung open, and Ginny froze. The very worst of her fears seemed to have materialised in front of her. It was all she could do not to stare, open-mouthed, in horror.

'Mr Bergovich?' she gulped.

The man bowed, stiffly, his face breaking into a polite smile. Short and balding, and as stocky as an all-in wrestler, she could scarcely believe her eyes. He looked about as approachable as a wild boar!

'Come,' he said, gesturing them inside with a podgy hand.

The room she found herself in was large and luxurious, well-lit by a central drop of lights. Among the elegant furnishings, the man couldn't have looked more out of place. He reminded her suddenly, sharply, of a rather nightmarish garden gnome.

Ginny blinked hard, but he didn't change, didn't get any better, and she turned quickly to Will for reassurance. But he wasn't even looking her way. Like her, his eyes were glued to the figure of their elderly host. Silently, Bergovich waved them towards a spindly-legged settee in richly-striped brocade, and without bothering with the niceties of asking first, he poured them each a glass of wine.

'Drink,' he insisted, pressing the glass into her hand.

Startled, Ginny lifted the ruby liquid obediently to her lips. Manners weren't exactly the man's strong point. But then, she reflected grimly, she'd known that before she came here.

'Mr Bergovich,' she began again.

Will appeared to have been struck speechless. He was perched on the edge of the sofa, twirling the wine glass mindlessly between his fingers, a look of disbelief on his face.

'Wait, wait,' their host insisted, his voice guttural and, with its strange foreign inflections, hard to understand.

Throwing them a brief smile, purely for politeness' sake, he went back to pour another glass of wine, this time for himself. Then he took a seat. Ginny had to pinch herself to make sure it was actually happening. How could she possibly reason with this man? He didn't even speak English.

'Mr Bergovich,' Will spoke at last, his voice far from firm, 'you know why we're here.'

But the man vehemently shook his head.

'Nah . . . no,' he interrupted, correcting his English pronunciation with ponderous care. 'Drink first, business later.'

He nodded again, and they stared at each other in silence. Ginny bit her lip hard. A nervous giggle was threatening to engulf her, and she had to struggle to fight it down.

'Please,' she said and turned to Will, a shaky note beginning to insert itself into her voice, 'can't we get on?'

'I've tried,' he returned, shrugging.

'Well, try again,' she said quickly. 'Really, Will, we can't just sit here, looking at each other.'

'Give it another five minutes,' he muttered sheepishly.

Ginny shook her head in mounting disbelief. What on earth was the matter with him? He was sitting there, mute, staring down at the glass in his hands. No wonder Bergovich ran rings around him. He looked beaten already.

'Will,' she prompted, 'I'm sure Mr Bergovich is a very busy man, and we shouldn't take up too much of his time.'

'Very true,' a deep voice said, and a tall figure strode into the room.

The newcomer was dark and unsmiling, well over six feet tall, with a ruggedly handsome face and the muscular build of an athlete. Everything about the man was expensive, as if he was only used to the very best. The suit he wore was grey and impeccably cut, encasing his powerful frame like a glove, and as he moved there was a glint of gold from the inch or so of white silk cuff at his wrists.

'Aleksander Bergovich,' he introduced himself.

Shock rendered Ginny temporarily speechless. She could only stare with dilated eyes at the haughty apparition that had suddenly presented itself. Please God, let it not be true, she stammered silently to herself. The garden gnome was easier to deal with than this formidable-looking man!

'But I thought . . . ' she began without thinking, her voice distinctly shaky.

'That Sergei was me,' the newcomer answered for her, the faintest hint of surprise in his tone. 'I'm sorry if you misunderstood,' he continued smoothly, 'but I am Aleksander Bergovich. Sergei is one of my factory managers. I had to ask him to entertain you, since I was taking an important call from home. I can only apologise for not greeting you myself.'

She stared up at the man, and he raised a dark brow in her direction. He certainly didn't look apologetic, rather the reverse, in fact. There was a commanding air about him she found just a trifle disconcerting. Self-assured and compelling, he personified all the power and purpose of a highly successful man very used to having his own way.

Uneasily, a hand crept up to her throat. She couldn't kid herself here. Bergovich didn't exactly appear the most promising of bargaining partners. Convincing him was going to be no pushover.

'Will,' she whispered, dry-mouthed.

Belatedly, he leaped to his feet, suddenly remembering himself, and he thrust out a hand towards his host.

'William Shepherd,' he announced, 'I believe we've spoken before, on the telephone.'

'Yes,' Bergovich broke in, 'I believe we have.'

He didn't like Will at all, that much was obvious. With a faintly disparaging expression, he looked the young man up and down, his chiselled features set like granite. Ginny swallowed hard. Will had really put her on the spot this time.

'You did agree to see us,' she broke in, her voice carefully calm, drawing his attention to herself.

Bergovich turned at once, his eyes holding hers for a timeless moment. It was her turn to be looked over, very slowly, and Ginny breathed hard under the watchful scrutiny. Instinctively, she lifted her chin, facing his stare.

'And who might you be?' he queried.

'My name is Virginia Eve,' she declared. 'Mr Shepherd's secretary.'

'Really?'

Bergovich took a step towards her, and before she realised what he was up to, his hand moved forward and grasped her fingers firmly in his.

'Well, good evening, Miss Eve,' he

murmured, and he raised her wrist to brush it lightly with his lips in the age-old gesture of chivalry.

For some unaccountable reason, colour touched Ginny's cheeks with scarlet. Hastily, she snatched her hand away.

'Good evening, Mr Bergovich,' she responded, meeting his eyes, her face a carefully composed mask.

Did he really imagine she was one of those silly women who found such affectations flattering? Stiffly, she held herself erect, but he merely smiled, his eyes still exploring her face with obvious appreciation.

'So lovely,' he breathed, 'such bone structure, with skin like cream. And those eyes,' he added softly.

He said something rapidly in his own tongue, throwing the words over his shoulder towards his balding henchman, and the man laughed aloud. It wasn't difficult to guess what they were discussing, and her face whitened. She recognised his type, only too well. His women were mere decorations, gracing his arm, there for his benefit. A flash of that film-star smile, a touch of practised charm, was more than enough to keep them in tow. Did he honestly harbour the notion that she was the same?

She shrugged. So what? Let him think what he likes. He would soon learn differently.

'Don't you think we should be getting on

with the evening's business?' she said with icy dignity, turning frigid dark eyes to search the dark, compelling depth of his own. 'After all, we have a lot to get through.'

'Surely business can wait for a moment,' he broke in softly, 'while we have another drink.'

Ginny didn't reply, as the words stuck in her throat. She didn't want to drink with the hateful man. But Will was quick to respond.

'Of course it can,' he broke in at once.

Bergovich threw him an icy look, and Will's voice died immediately into silence. But the man removed the glass from Will's fingers, taking it over to the drinks' cabinet to refill. Ginny refused the offer of a refill herself, her expression strictly neutral.

'I really think we should be getting on.'

'Maybe you're right,' Bergovich conceded at last, and, carrying his glass with him, he gestured towards a half-open door.

Silently, they followed him through, into a small room. It was obviously a study, with a briefcase lying on a table beside several piles of neatly-ordered files. A telephone was prominent, together with a portable laptop computer, all set and ready to use.

'Please, have a seat,' he invited, waving a hand, and they gathered together around the table. 'Now, Mr Shepherd,' Bergovich continued smoothly, 'let me hear what you have to say.'

Ginny thought the hour went well. Once the

business was started, Bergovich was crisp and curt, not missing a thing, but she'd briefed Will to the point of saturation and it was paying off. He put forward their package with practised ease, even managing to field his host's most penetrating questions with a fair degree of aplomb. Fortunately, the man asked nothing Ginny hadn't thought of first, and she could sit in virtual silence, passing Will the notes as he needed them.

The minutes rolled by without any nasty shocks, and Ginny started to breathe more easily. They might get away with it after all.

'This is very impressive.'

Bergovich frowned, his eyes flicking over the careful lines of figures.

'Why haven't I seen anything like this before?'

'Well,' Will stammered, at a loss, and Ginny leaped in to fill the gap.

'Will had shown you only the briefest outline of the firm's plans,' she put in at once. 'Now, he wants you to consider the final package.'

Her sudden intrusion into the conversation obviously took Bergovich by surprise. He turned his dark gaze towards her.

'You speak for him?' he queried.

'I'm his secretary,' she replied, her expression calm, professional. 'It's my job to keep Mr Shepherd's material at his fingertips.'

'Really?' Bergovich replied. 'I am surprised.

I thought a secretary's job was merely to type and take orders, and make the tea, of course.'

The silence round the table was deafening. Ginny took in a deep, hissing breath. The condescending beast, trying to put her in her place! But it took only seconds for her to compose her features and turn to face the man.

'Oh, no,' she said sweetly, 'I'm more of a partner to Mr Shepherd than that. You must be thinking of the office juniors straight out of school.'

'No, I was thinking about secretaries,' he corrected at once.

The broad shoulders lifted and he inclined his head, dark eyes resting thoughtfully on the upturned oval of her face.

'And you are old enough to give this advice?' he queried politely.

Ginny threw him a scathing look.

'I am twenty-two!' she stated stiffly.

'Mm, you look younger.'

'I am quite old enough to do my job correctly.'

'In my country,' Bergovich went on, totally unperturbed, 'a woman like you, so young, so very lovely, would find her satisfactions, her rôle in life, in making her man happy, not in giving advice in the business place.'

Ginny's temperature shot up a notch or two, until she could have almost sworn she could actually feel the steam coming out of her ears.

To keep the polite smile fixed on her face almost killed her, but she would not give him the pleasure of seeing her lose her cool.

'But that attitude belongs in the Middle Ages,' she murmured, her tone deliberately smooth. 'It has no role in modern times in this country.'

'Then this must be a very sorry place.'

His tone was casual, his English perfect, with only the slightest trace of an accent, but it was enough to remind them Bergovich hailed from a different culture from theirs, so Ginny held her tongue. Besides, she couldn't afford to upset him now, not when they were so close to success.

'We all have our customs, Mr Bergovich,' she conceded softly.

She was treated to another long stare. His eyes held hers, darkly intent, for what seemed like an age. Then he nodded.

'Of course,' he agreed.

For the next half-hour, Ginny's patience was sorely tried. She had to sit by quietly, her face impassive, listening to the arguments going back and forth, over her head, while Will set out her proposals for her. And he was taking an age to come to the point. Restlessly, she stirred in her seat, biting her lip to keep silent. Left to herself, she would have closed the deal when they were ahead, but Will was still pressing on, going round and round in circles in his efforts to please. Balefully, she glared over the table at him until he finally took the hint.

'So, do we have an agreement?' he enquired at last, his eyes hopeful.

'Maybe,' Bergovich conceded, 'but I need a few days to think it over. Maybe we could meet for dinner, after the week-end, when I've had time to go through all the proposals.'

'Of course, of course,' Will gabbled agreement. 'You won't regret it. This will be good for us both, you'll see.'

But when he tried to grasp Bergovich by the hand, the man shrugged it away.

'Better for you, I think, my young friend,' he stated in cutting tones. 'I have no reason to fear as you do. But it is an interesting package,' he added grudgingly, 'so I will be in touch. Now, though, if you don't mind, I am a very busy man.'

It was a dismissal. But Ginny had had more than enough of the man for one evening, and was only too glad to put some distance between them. Without another word, she collected the papers together and positively rammed them into her briefcase.

'Come on, Will,' she urged, 'let's get away before he changes his mind.'

Will took her to dinner, just as he promised, but Ginny was unsettled. The evening hadn't been the success she'd hoped for, and she could only pick at her spaghetti, pushing it aimlessly round her plate with her fork.

'Well, at least he didn't say no,' Will whispered.

'He didn't say yes, either,' she reminded him.

He was frowning, anxiety etched deep about his eyes. Slowly, she reached up, smoothing the lines away with gentle fingertips, her expression tender with love. How different he was from the hateful Bergovich.

'We'll come through this,' she promised, and for the first time in days, a kind of weary peace filled his face.

'Together?' he queried.

'Together,' she whispered back.

CHAPTER TWO

That night, Ginny took a long time falling asleep. As soon as her head touched the pillow, her mind was invaded by a swarthy face with a dark, compelling smile—the face of Aleksander Bergovich. Then sleep just fled.

Aleksander Bergovich was the kind of man she generally avoided. She couldn't pretend she liked him, respected him, even. The mere thought of that condescending face positively turned her stomach. Finally, though, she did manage to drop off for a couple of hours, but she was up and about again at the crack of dawn, pale and unsettled from lack of sleep.

Will was coming for lunch so with a whole morning to get through, Ginny turned her mind to cooking something special. Will loved fresh trout prepared in her own white wine sauce, and she decided on that. Preparation was its secret, and she spent hours getting it ready.

The trout was done to a turn when Will arrived. He sniffed appreciatively at the delicious smells drifting in from the kitchen.

'Something nice?' he queried, smiling.

'Wait and see,' she teased, her face quite straight.

But his smile was far too infectious to keep up the pretence for long. Wickedly, he grinned, swinging her into his arms to press his lips warmly against hers.

'Tell me at once, woman,' he quipped.

Suddenly, she felt so content with life, so safe again, and she melted against him, enjoying his strength, his familiar warmth against her.

'Oh, Will, I do love you.'

'And don't you ever forget it,' he replied, 'even for that character, Bergovich. I can imagine him being attractive to some women.'

His face was sulky, like that of a small boy who couldn't get his own way, and she had to hide a smile. He was so sweet when he was jealous.

'Don't be silly,' she warned, eyes sparkling, 'or you won't get your trout for lunch. I'll give it to the cat instead.'

They ate their meal in silence, just enjoying the food, not needing to speak. But sooner or later, Aleksander Bergovich managed to insinuate his unwelcome way into the conversation.

'What worries me most,' Ginny said, whisking the remains of the trout away and replacing it with a strawberry cheesecake, 'is what we'll do if the man asks for more. We've stretched our resources to the limit already, but I can't imagine anyone else offering him such a good deal, and within his time limits. So, maybe we're in with a chance.'

'You are, you mean,' Will said. 'Bergovich

certainly had an eye for you.'

Wryly, she shook her head, half-annoyed by the words, but half-amused at the same time.

'Now you really are being silly,' she said. 'Eat up so I can clear away.'

He did, every scrap of it, with such relish she had to hide a rueful smile.

'Now,' he whispered, when the dishes were washed and they were relaxing on the sofa, 'I can think of much better ways of spending Saturday afternoon than worrying about Aleksander Bergovich.'

He drew her closer and captured her lips in a tender kiss. She pushed him back with a half-smothered sigh.

'Enough,' she whispered. 'We have to get this business sorted out.'

He wasn't best pleased.

'Of course,' he snapped, 'let's get back to Bergovich. I'm not so sure you don't fancy him, after all.'

She knew it was only his jealousy speaking, but she sighed just the same. If she'd managed to get this far without resorting to histrionics, surely he could do the same.

'I love you,' she said, her words insistent, 'and I always will. Surely, you know that.'

She went into the kitchen and put on the kettle. She was used to Will's occasional sulks by now, and she could usually cope with them well enough. But this was getting on her nerves. How could he imagine she fancied a man like Aleksander Bergovich?

'Ginny?'

He came up close behind her, squeezing her waist lovingly.

'Don't be angry with me,' he pleaded, 'it's just that, well, I've got something to tell you, and I don't know how. I've been trying, all afternoon, but I can't seem to find the right words.'

She knew from his expression it wasn't good news. Shaken, she turned towards him, her face paper white.

'Bergovich has contacted you? Already?' she asked.

He couldn't meet her eyes. Wretchedly, he nodded.

'And he isn't interested in the package?' she queried.

It couldn't be true, not after all their work.

'Oh, no, not that.'

Will smiled, a strange, humourless smile.

'What then?'

Her voice was faint, scarcely audible, and she searched his face with troubled eyes.

'If you give me a moment, I'll tell you,' Will returned, just a trifle shortly. 'He wants the firm to put on a reception, to meet the directors, see the company for himself.'

'But what's wrong with that?' she queried, her eyes shining. 'You can welcome him officially as the new foreign partner.'

'It's not quite that simple,' he broke in,

struggling to keep his voice steady. 'He won't sign the contracts until after the reception.'

'But he will sign afterwards?' she asked, her expression thoughtful.

'So he says.'

'Then we have to go along with it.'

Will should have looked relieved, very relieved, and so he did. But there was a definite shadow of doubt in his face as well.

'But that's not all,' he responded slowly.

'So, what else does he want?'

'To see you again!'

The words almost exploded between them. Thunderstruck, Ginny stared over at him.

'See me again?' she repeated incredulously.

Her mind blanked, simply refusing to take it in.

'You heard,' he retorted, somewhat peevishly, as if he imagined it was somehow her fault.

Who did Bergovich think he was? This was real life, not some fanciful, Hollywood movie. It was all she could do not to laugh.

'Then he can see me again, at the party.'

She grinned. The whole idea was preposterous.

'What if he wants more than that?'

'Don't be silly.' She laughed, reaching up to plant a kiss on his cheek.

'You go ahead, my love, and arrange his precious reception. I can take care of myself.'

So he went along with it, and the

management positively leaped at the idea of a party. They'd been looking for a way to show off their new developments in Eastern Europe, a grand way that made them look good, and an expensive reception seemed the very thing to do it. Strings were pulled to hire the ballroom at one of the best hotels in the capital, a converted country mansion just a little way out of town, with a breathtaking view across the river.

'It's amazing what you can achieve with money behind you,' Ginny commented as caterers, florists and wine merchants fell into line.

'Yes,' Will breathed, 'and if this deal comes off, we'll be right up there with the best of them.'

'One day at a time,' she teased, digging him in the ribs.

By the end of the month, literally hundreds of invitations had been sent out, and the entire firm was agog with the news. Only one person in the place wasn't living excitedly for the day, and that person, of course, was Ginny. Normally, she would have loved the chance to swirl round the dance floor, clasped in Will's arms, but Will himself wasn't making things very easy for her. He was getting increasingly agitated, certain that Bergovich would never secure the contract, not just like that. He simply couldn't believe it.

'What if he wants something in return,' he

insisted. 'Time with you?'

But his fears were just too theatrical, too melodramatic for real life. Ginny did her best to reassure him. Bergovich was a businessman. Surely, commonsense told her, that's all he'd be interested in.

Will was calling early to escort her to the celebrations on the night, and with a half-smothered sigh, she turned her attention to getting ready. Carefully, she outlined her mouth with a delicate shade of soft red, but her velvety eyes with their fringes of thick, dark lashes needed little to enhance their beauty. They glowed like jewels in the creamy oval of her face.

Her new dress, bought especially for the occasion, was waiting for her, featuring the slenderest of ribbon straps, and a fitted waist. In it, she seemed as delicately fragile as finest porcelain.

She caught her hair into a soft knot on the top of her head, allowing a few shining tendrils to float loose about her ears and the nape of her slender neck. Ear-rings, swinging like long silver tassels, were slipped through her ears, and then, as a final touch, Ginny clasped an antique locket around her neck. It was a family heirloom she'd inherited from an aunt, and it hung delicately on its fine silver chain. With a careful look she inspected herself in the full-length mirror. Her heart might be hammering like a drum, but no-one would ever know it, she looked so cool and elegant.

Will's face was spellbound as she opened the door to him.

'Do I look all right?' she enquired, dropping her eyes demurely.

'You look wonderful in that dress.'

Very gently, he kissed her, deepening the embrace quickly as she melted against him. But with a tantalising smile, she slid out of his arms.

'We can't be late,' she insisted, though she would rather have stayed at home with Will than have to meet Bergovich at this most glittering reception.

'I've got something for you,' Will said.

He pushed a ribboned box into her hands, and with a small cry of delight, she pulled the wrapping away. It was a single gardenia, snowy white and heavy with fragrance. He had remembered!

'My favourite,' she breathed.

'I know,' he said, and carefully, he slipped the delicate blossom into her hair. 'There,' he added softly, 'just perfect.'

Will picked up her silvery wrap, folding it gently round her shoulders as a bell sounded at the door. Abruptly, his face darkened.

'Are you sure now?' he whispered. 'Do you still want to go?'

'I'll be fine,' she murmured, reaching up to smooth the lines of anxiety from around his mouth.

'Then the taxi's here. It's time to go.'

The hotel stood, aloof and exclusive, in its own stately grounds on the banks of the Thames, and she caught her first glimpse of it with decidedly mixed feelings. The taxi turned off the road, crossing an ornate bridge over the river, to pull up in front of the impressive façade. Already, the place was crowded, but they didn't join any of the little knots of people making their way inside. Will avoided them all. He helped Ginny out of the car, gripping her firmly by the elbow, and he escorted her swiftly up the shallow flight of stone steps towards the wide front door.

It was warm inside, and buzzing with conversation. Her wrap was whisked away at once, together with Will's outdoor coat, and before she even had time to think, they were announced by the dark-coated Master of Ceremonies and ushered into the crowded ballroom.

The sight that met their eyes was magnificent. The room was huge, lit by glittering chandeliers spilling down from the ceiling like crystal waterfalls. Banks of fresh flowers, glowing with colour, filled the warm air with their perfume. The dancing didn't start until after dinner, and the floor was filled with people chatting, mingling, wine glasses clasped between their fingertips. Here and there, waiters flitted among them, trays full of drinks.

'This way,' Will whispered, urging her towards the group of top management officials standing close by.

Ginny grimaced. She didn't enjoy their company as much as Will evidently did. The men were elderly, and far too conscious of their own importance for her liking. Their expensively-clad wives with their cold eyes and fixed smiles weren't much better!

'Do we have to?' she whispered, but it was too late, as Will was already shaking hands with Thomas King, the firm's managing director.

'Glad to see you, my boy,' he said. 'You should be proud. This is all down to you.'

His eyes fixed on Ginny with a smile that was probably meant to look paternal, and he patted her arm as if he considered he had every right to touch her. Discreetly, she drew away, her smile fixed to her lips.

'Ah, Miss Eve,' he leered, 'you look very pretty tonight, very pretty indeed. I only wish I was thirty years younger, then I'd give Shepherd a real run for his money.'

'Give a younger man a chance,' Will broke in, a trifle too brightly in Ginny's opinion.

He needn't be quite so effusive. It was the only thing they ever really argued about, King's roving eyes and his too-hot, too-familiar hands. She didn't think she should have to put up with them, whatever Will said.

'Ah, well.' King smiled. 'Off you go and

enjoy yourselves.'

'Has the guest of honour arrived?' Will queried.

'Oh, Bergovich? Not yet.'

At that precise moment, the voice of the Master of Ceremonies rang out in solemn importance above the general hum of conversation.

'Mr Aleksander Bergovich and Mr Sergei Ivanovitch Bounin.'

For a second, the room fell quiet, and all eyes were drawn to the short flight of steps leading down from the door. Then Bergovich walked in, and the silence was complete. Pausing in the doorway, he glanced down into the vast ballroom, well aware that every single eye was upon him. He seemed to fill the room with his presence. And, Ginny noted sourly, he didn't improve on second acquaintance. There was still that touch of condescension about his mouth which she remembered so well, and the look of cool superiority in his dark eyes she found so disconcerting.

But the man was attractive just the same; she couldn't deny it. He had an air about him, a compelling, physical presence that fluttered every female heart in the room. With a slight bow he acknowledged the interest of the assembled guests. Silently, she watched him approach, and with just the slightest touch of cynicism, she noted Thomas King strut forward, puffed with importance, to clasp the man by the hand.

'Welcome, welcome,' he fussed.

Will stood still as Bergovich stepped forward, stretching out his hand, his face welcoming. He took Will's hand, if only very briefly, then turning slightly, his eyes rested on the slender figure of Ginny. Silently, she stood before him, head held elegantly erect, shimmering against the colourful background. With one brow raised, he took a step towards her.

'Good evening, Miss Eve,' Bergovich murmured. 'May I say, you're looking quite exquisite tonight.'

'Thank you,' she said, but the response was purely automatic.

She wasn't taken in for a minute by this display of synthetic charm. She despised him for what he was doing to Will, and all the compliments in the world wouldn't change that. With a smile, he lifted her reluctant hand in his, bending over it to press his lips warmly against her wrist. Politely, his mouth brushed her skin, softly, lingering against the silky surface. Its butterfly touch sent tiny sparks of fire leaping the entire length of her spine. Startled, her eyes shot up to meet his.

'Perhaps we'll meet again, later this evening?' he queried.

Eyes burning with dark fire gazed deep into hers, holding her captive beneath a long, glittering look. The man was an animal, an animal, she told herself fiercely, and a wild one at that. With a shaky smile, she moistened her bottom lip with the tip of her tongue.

'Perhaps,' she conceded at last.

'I'll look forward to it,' he promised.

Gently, his long fingers released their hold, and with another velvety smile, he stepped away.

'Until later, Miss Eve,' he said.

A grinning Thomas King immediately claimed him, and he was hustled away with Sergei in his wake. Ginny watched them go, feeling decidedly flustered. She knew her cheeks were crimson, and her entire body was bathed in a sudden, unaccountable warmth.

'Smarmy devil,' Will snarled.

'Don't be silly,' she returned.

But she knew her colour had deepened even further under Will's furious stare, and somehow, she couldn't bring herself to meet his eyes.

'It's not me who's being silly,' Will insisted, and his voice was harsh as he added, 'I know what I saw. I thought you didn't like him.'

He was definitely sulking now, she told herself, imagining things that weren't there. She loved him. Other men didn't even enter her scheme of things. Couldn't he see that?

'Will,' she said, 'do you trust me?'

'Yes, but . . . '

'Then there aren't any buts, are there?'

Her voice was low, decisive, and slowly, he

shook his head.

'I know,' he agreed, his eyes dull with misery, 'but he could charm ducks off water. Maybe he'll do the same to you.'

'He could never do that,' she returned gently. 'Never. I despise Bergovich, despise everything he stands for.'

'Maybe,' Will broke in, 'but I can't bear to think about it, you and him.'

'Then don't,' she insisted. 'Believe me, it will never be me and him, not now, not ever. It's me and you, and don't you ever forget it. So let's go over and join our friends. I think we could both do with a drink.'

Dinner was served in the adjoining room, and Ginny almost enjoyed it. Bergovich was seated at the head of the top table, and if she didn't look too far to the left, he was just far enough away to miss. All through the endless introductions, she sat, hiding a less than enthusiastic face, and when Thomas King announced that he hoped the association would be a long one, she even managed to join in the applause.

After that, it was fairly easy to turn her back on Bergovich, blocking him totally from view. The food was delicious, taking up all her attention, and by the time dessert was finally served, she was almost completely relaxed.

'And when are you two naming the day?' a female colleague asked, tossing back long, blonde hair and throwing Ginny a sly grin.

'Soon, maybe.'

She laughed back, her eyes on Will's smiling face.

The music began, and with a dreamy smile, Ginny tapped her foot gently in time to the rhythm. She would enjoy dancing with Will, holding him close.

'May I have the pleasure of this dance, Miss Eve?' a deep voice said, and she turned, every nerve in her body suddenly jumping like mad.

Without even looking up, she knew it was Bergovich.

'Of course, thank you, Mr Bergovich,' she stammered.

'Please, let us not be so formal,' he demurred. 'My name is Aleksander, but my English friends tend to call me Alex.'

'Thank you, Alex,' she intoned obediently, and she rose to take his hand.

She could have sworn the room fell silent as he escorted her out on to the floor. Certainly, every eye was turned towards them, but the faces were just a blur in her consciousness. All she was aware of was the powerful figure looming at her side.

'Miss Eve,' he said, sketching a brief bow, and with another gleaming smile, he gathered her into his arms.

He danced superbly, with an obvious lightness and grace, and they moved together in perfect time to the music. She was embarrassingly conscious of the strength of the arms about her, the power of the muscular body close to her own. What if Will was right? The man seemed huge, invincible, as if nothing on earth would stand in his way if he decided he wanted something.

'Miss Eve,' he murmured.

'Ginny,' she corrected automatically.

'Oh, I prefer Miss Eve,' he said, smiling. 'The name is so apt. Eve, the ultimate temptress.'

Ginny could think of no possible answer to that. Silently, she prayed for a breeze from somewhere, anywhere, to cool her glowing cheeks. Temptress, indeed! He could forget that idea. She'd just as soon tempt Thomas King!

They danced twice more, her eyes fixed to the buttons on his white shirt front. Grimly, she pulled herself together, and with the sweetest of smiles, she launched into an unending flow of inconsequential small talk. She'd show him he didn't worry the likes of her. She discussed the weather, and what he thought of England. Smiling, she tossed her head, nodded, touching on every topic of conversation she could think of, until she finally ran out of things to say.

'Isn't it warm in here?' she finished at last.

He paused at once in their dancing, his face a picture of polite concern.

'So, shall we go for a walk on the patio?' he enquired softly.

Startled, she glanced up, giving him a small, insipid smile. Why hadn't she thought before she spoke? The last thing on earth she wanted was to be alone with the wretched man.

'I . . . er . . . don't know,' she began, stumbling over the words in her confusion, but his brows shot up at her hesitation.

'Really, Miss Eve,' he whispered, mouth twisting in mocking amusement, 'do you believe I have designs on you? Nothing is further from the truth. Delectable as you are, I can assure you, you will be quite safe. I am not so overcome by your beauty that your honour is at stake.'

Colour shot into her face, and she threw up her head, pale skin alight with mortification. There was no need for him to be quite so condescending.

'I was thinking no such thing,' she defended hotly.

'No?' he queried.

'No,' she insisted, eyes flashing jewel bright with defiance.

'Then let us go outside,' he said.

He took her arm, and with a tense smile, she allowed him to lead her away from the floor at the next break in the music. It was crowded by now, full of swaying couples, but their escape route was easy. People simply seemed to melt out of his way.

Outside, the night was calm and beautiful. The patio was cool after the ballroom, cool and quiet, enclosed in a trailing mantle of greenery. The fresh, sweet scent touched the air with fragrance, and Ginny leaned on the stone balustrade, looking out over the moonwashed garden. A silvery path stretched out across the lawn, winding its magical way beneath the autumnal trees to vanish into the shadows.

Alex appeared at her elbow, a glass of sparkling champagne held out in his hand. Sighing, she accepted. Sipping it gave her something to do. Whatever the man said, she still didn't trust him an inch, and she edged along the balustrade, doing her best to leave a decent space between them.

'You like the garden?' he queried, following her maddeningly.

'Yes,' she agreed in a faintly strangled voice.

'Personally, I've seen better,' he commented gravely.

'Really?' she returned, refusing to be drawn.

'Really,' he replied. 'Damask roses in the East, with fountains splashing over marble tiles, or frangipani and jasmine, heady with perfume, lifting in the breeze on whitewashed, Mediterranean terraces. Need I go on?'

'No,' she snapped.

A cruel little breeze out of nowhere suddenly ruffled her hair, and he lifted a hand to smooth a wayward tendril back into place. His fingers were strong, lean, almost possessive, and she shivered at their touch.

'Cold?' he enquired.

'A little.'

Gently, he removed the glass from her fingers and placed it on the stone wall. Then he reached out to grip her waist, and he began to draw her to him. It took every ounce of her self-control not to push him away.

'Mr Bergovich . . . Alex,' she protested shakily, but he didn't stop.

He took her into his arms, holding her close, enfolding her gently against the wall of his chest. Breathlessly, she held herself erect, determined to stay calm. And why shouldn't she? After all, the man was only about to kiss her. She could certainly manage that. And kiss her he did. His lips moved against hers, warm and insistent. A warm tide of feeling flowed through her, and gasping, she tried to pull away. But his arms drew her closer still.

She closed her eyes, her breath caught, willing her pulses not to leap quite so traitorously. But his lips touched hers with a sweetness that melted her bones.

'Alex,' she murmured, still half-protesting, but again, he didn't stop.

The kiss lingered and her heart began to race, its beat pounding like a drum. Will had never kissed her like this. No-one had ever kissed her like this, sending her so hot and dazed and shaky. Instinctively, she clung closer, waiting for the world to rock back on to its axis again. His hand reached up, tender and warm, cradling the nape of her neck.

For a long, timeless moment, she stared upwards, meeting his gaze, unable to move, scarcely able to breathe. In the muted light, the shadows threw his strong features into unsmiling relief, his mouth a vague curve, his eyes gleaming and soft in the darkness.

'May I escort you home, Miss Eve?' he whispered into her ear.

It was a straightforward question, so unexpected it momentarily threw her, and all she could do was nod her head, mutely, all words temporarily lost. But gradually her pulse evened, her breathing steadied out, and with chin high, she followed the tall figure back to the ballroom. She even managed a smile when he brought her wrap.

'Thank you,' she murmured.

Aware of all the curious eyes upon them, she allowed him to slip the shimmering wrap about her naked shoulders, and when he offered his arm, she slipped her small hand unhesitatingly into the crook of his elbow. Then together, they left the hotel.

CHAPTER THREE

It had started to rain, not much at first, just a fine drizzle hanging in the air like mist. But it was enough. Maybe it wasn't quite an omen, Ginny thought cynically, but it came close. The summer was well and truly over.

Clutching her firmly by the arm, Alex escorted her quickly down the floodlit steps. At a lift of his hand, a black monster of a car came whispering out of the night, as if by magic. He flung open the passenger door without so much as a word, and quietly she slid inside.

'Thank you,' she acknowledged automatically.

He nodded, but he didn't reply. He was too busy digging in his inside pocket to find his wallet. But that suited Ginny just fine. What could she say to him? Why was she there? For Will? For the contract? Because she wanted to be? She didn't know for sure herself.

The car smelled faintly of fine leather and wax polish, and she sank appreciatively back into the luxurious upholstery. Almost at once, the young attendant slid out of the driver's seat, relinquishing the keys into Alex's hand with an envious little smile.

'Your car, sir,' he said.

Nodding, Alex accepted them, slipping the

man an unobtrusive tip in return. But he didn't smile back.

'See that Mr Bounin gets a taxi back to the hotel,' he instructed briefly.

Ginny gave him her address, then she turned away to gaze through the window. Outside, the neon lights of the city flashed by and she watched them pass with unblinking eyes. The journey seemed to take longer than she ever remembered before, but finally they reached her home, and Alex eased the car into the allotted space in the basement carpark.

'Would you like to come in for a coffee?' she enquired.

'Of course,' he rejoined with a slight shrug of his shoulders. 'I wouldn't miss your coffee for the world.'

He was out of the car in a second, his tall figure towering above her. They reached her door in silence, and with fumbling fingers, she pushed the key in the lock. Alex was right behind her, following her into the hall, and she watched as he removed his coat.

It was a trifle chilly so she lit the gas fire, and the flickering flames of the artificial log fire brought the room warmly to life. Usually, she loved sitting with Will in its romantic half light, but not tonight. Tonight, she played safe, switching on all the lamps, flicking them on one after another. Bergovich blinked, obviously surprised by the growing pools of light, but he didn't make any comment. He

46

arranged his long body in one of the easy chairs and, picking up a nearby magazine, he began to flick through its pages.

Thankfully, Ginny left him to it, glad to escape into the empty silence of the kitchen. Maybe Will was wrong, and all the man wanted to discuss with her were the wretched contracts. But she wasn't lowering her guard just yet. He hadn't quite gained her trust.

It didn't take long to make the coffee, and she loaded the silver pot on to a tray with two of her best china cups. Alex leaped to his feet the moment she reappeared, lifting the heavy tray from her outstretched hands. Deftly, he slid it on to the glass-topped table standing alongside the settee.

'Cream and sugar?' he queried, taking over the task and helping himself liberally to both.

'Just cream,' she replied with studied calm, accepting the offered cup.

Secretly, she was just a little surprised to see how readily he managed such a mundane domestic task, and he smiled at the look of disbelief which flitted across her face.

'I have not always been a man of means,' he informed her smoothly.

She took up a solitary position on the sofa, not wanting to sit too close, but maddeningly, Alex didn't take the hint. The cushions dipped alarmingly as they took his weight, and his muscular frame eased down beside her.

'Have you been in London before, Mr

Bergovich?' she queried in a somewhat strained tone.

She had to say something, anything, to fill the yawning silence.

'My dear, you must learn to call me Alex,' he countered at once.

She didn't want to call him Alex, but she could hardly tell him that. So she took a deep breath to steady herself, and started again.

'Have you been in London before, then, Alex?' she conceded, forcing a stiff smile to her lips, and he nodded.

'Some eight or nine times,' he informed her. 'But,' he added with a small half-smile, 'my great-grandfather happened to be English, so I grew up knowing something about the place.'

Ginny was intrigued in spite of herself. She suddenly realised how little she knew of this man, except what Will had told her. She threw him a sideways look, her attention caught, and he nodded across at her.

'Ah, I see I have aroused your interest at last,' he noted, genuine amusement glinting in his dark eyes.

He chatted easily as they finished their coffee, smoothly filling in the details of his family story.

'So,' he finished, 'it was one of those family fables, the love story of a young English captain serving in the Great War and his beautiful, Russian peasant girl.'

'Peasant girl!' Ginny interrupted, sharp-eyed, objecting at once to the derogatory expression.

'Such were the times,' he conceded, 'but she was young, dark-eyed and very pretty, so the captain stayed, married and fathered five strong sons.'

'Really? I didn't realise you were Russian,' she commented.

'And you'd be right,' he allowed with a nod. 'My grandfather, the youngest of the five, finally settled in Estonia. That's where my mother was born, and later on, myself.'

'You're quite a mixture.'

'Russian, English, Estonian.' He shrugged. 'But mostly the latter. I wish I could tell you I came from more aristocratic origins, but sadly it isn't so.'

She returned the shrug, with a small, elegant lift to her slender shoulders.

'There's no need to apologise for that,' she responded, though she had the distinct feeling he wasn't telling her all the truth—his family probably owned half of Estonia! 'There's nothing aristocratic about me, either,' she confessed with a smile. 'I'm just an ordinary, working woman myself.'

His brows rose, and he regarded her with openly incredulous eyes.

'Ordinary?' he queried. 'Surely not! I find that very hard to believe.'

'Oh, but I am,' she insisted, ignoring the sudden depth in his tone. 'My father's a bank manager, and my mother teaches in the local primary school, five-year-olds to be exact.'

Her words died away to nothing. Alex was looking at her in a manner that brought a delicate flush to her cheeks, his gaze resting on the curve of her shoulder and the creamy column of her throat. Turning a carefully composed face towards him, Ginny threw him a brief smile. Suddenly, it didn't seem the time or place for taking any chances.

'Well, I mustn't keep you,' she said. 'I'll get your coat.'

She got to her feet just as he leaned her way, managing to avoid the embrace she was sure was coming. She escaped into the hall. Quickly, she reached up to lift down his coat, but a hand reached over her shoulder.

'Miss Eve . . . Ginny . . . '

Alex's voice murmured into her ear, and she turned to find he had followed her. Her heart sank. He lifted her chin, bringing her body close to his, and she knew without a shadow of a doubt that Alex was going to kiss her. His lips found hers, lightly at first.

Every instinct yelled out to stop him, to pull away, but she was quivering like a leaf, unable to move, gripped by a sensation far too sweet to resist. This couldn't be happening! Swiftly, she twisted against him, struggling to draw away. With a sigh, he finally released her from his arms.

'My dear, what on earth is the matter?' he

50

asked.

He was standing in front of her, so casually that anger consumed her, and without pausing to think, her hand flew up and she smacked him, sharply, across his unsmiling face. Alex took a jerky step backwards. The mark of her hand showed red against his dark skin.

'Take care,' he warned. 'You go too far.'

'You asked for it,' she snapped, still shaking inwardly.

'You blame a man for kissing you?'

'I blame a man for not stopping when I say no.'

'But I did stop,' he stated coldly. 'I stopped the moment you said it.'

She was suddenly confused. Why had she reacted so wildly?

'I thought . . . I thought you weren't listening,' she put in quickly.

'You thought I intended to go further, in exchange for my signature on Shepherd's contract,' he contradicted grimly.

She couldn't pretend any longer. She didn't even try. She was too tired, too confused, too overwrought to keep it up.

'Yes,' she confirmed, dropping her gaze downwards.

He scrutinised her again, silently, with appraising, hooded eyes, until she felt every nerve in her body on edge.

'What kind of man do you think I am?' he said softly. 'An uncivilised foreigner, no doubt,

51

from some godforsaken land. It may surprise you to know,' he continued, his voice bitingly harsh, 'that Estonia was once a centre of culture and sophistication, and we haven't forgotten it all. We may be impoverished now, but we are not completely without honour.'

'I didn't think you were,' she protested, somewhat taken aback by his accusations.

'You didn't think at all,' he snapped back. 'You didn't think about my feelings, or your own for that matter.'

'I don't know what you mean,' she stammered.

For a moment he didn't go on, his expression bleak, then the imperious mouth softened a little.

'My sweet, lovely Ginny,' he continued at last, 'I really don't think that you do. You have no idea, have you, what you've started tonight.'

'Started?' she queried, now truly nonplussed.

'Yes, started,' he affirmed softly. 'Surely you must have guessed how attracted I am to you. More than anything in the world,' he insisted, his voice a mere whisper, 'I want to hold you, kiss you, make you mine.'

His eyes roved over her upturned features with an expression that stopped her breath. No-one had ever looked at her quite like that before, and her heart seemed to race into overdrive. She didn't want to hear this.

'I thought you were a man of honour,' she

reminded him.

Hearing those words, flung so vehemently at him, Alex's lips twisted into a distinctly mocking line. Shrugging, he raised his brows.

'You should thank your lucky stars that I am,' he concurred. 'But, my dear Miss Eve, be honest for once,' he added, his eyes gleaming, 'it isn't my feelings you're so frightened of, is it? It's your own.'

Ginny had never heard anything so ludicrous. He might be attractive, physically attractive, but she hardly knew him. Besides, she wanted more from a man than a brief affair.

'Don't be ridiculous,' she broke in, cutting him short.

'Are you so sure?'

Doggedly, she met his eyes, still trying grimly to hang on to her dignity. But his gaze didn't waver, and the tell-tale surge of pink into her cheeks showed her confusion. Hotly, she remembered the sweet need he had aroused in her, and she flinched, more confused than ever.

'Haven't you forgotten something?' she demanded at last. 'I'm engaged to Will. I love him.'

He shrugged at that, obviously unconvinced.

'Of course, of course, we mustn't forget Mr Shepherd,' he allowed.

Lifting her chin, she met his eyes. But it was true. She loved Will. She wanted to marry him, live the rest of her life at his side. Nothing else mattered.

'I will never forget him,' she insisted softly.

'Prove it,' he put in at once.

Prove it? Ginny's eyes widened. What on earth did he mean by that?

'I don't need to prove anything,' she began haughtily.

'Oh, but you do,' he breathed. 'If you refuse, if you turn away now, you'll always wonder if I'm right. There will always be that niggle at the back of your mind, that you found me, Alex Bergovich, that arrogant foreigner, more attractive, more desirable than your precious Will Shepherd.'

'Never,' she retorted hotly.

'That's good,' he said suddenly, his voice very brisk, and she glanced up, completely taken aback.

'Good?' she questioned blankly.

What could he possibly mean by that? Alex gave a lift to his broad shoulders, throwing her a half-smile, smooth and very assured.

'Yes, good,' he replied, nodding. 'I'm going away, to Florence, on business, next week, and I need someone to keep me company.'

If he had physically struck her, Ginny couldn't have been more surprised. She could only gape over at him open-mouthed.

'You can't mean me,' she broke in, appalled.

What on earth was he talking about now?

'Why not you?' he queried, eyebrows raised

54

in a creditable imitation of surprise. 'I need a companion, at the theatre or for a meal.'

'And why should that interest me?' she parried carefully.

His brows rose, and he shrugged, his mouth curved in amusement.

'I thought you might like to see Florence,' he murmured, the words low and persuasive. 'It's a beautiful city, in a beautiful country. I'd like to share it with you. No strings. You have my word on that.'

'And I can believe it?'

'Absolutely.'

She still didn't understand, and the surprised expression on her young features showed it only too plainly.

'But there must be plenty of women around ready to jump at the chance,' she stammered.

'True,' he agreed, 'but they don't have quite the same appeal.'

It was crazy to feel so vulnerable, crazy, but nonetheless true. Her heart was thudding under his smiling gaze, and she could hardly breathe.

'I don't feel the same way,' she managed to say at last.

'Maybe not,' he stated softly, 'but I'll take the chance,' he added smoothly. 'I need a companion, a woman I can escort around Florence.'

'But not me,' she broke in. 'Will would never agree.'

For several seconds, Alex regarded her in silence, his eyes holding more than a hint of cynicism in their dark depths. Then, very gently, he lifted a hand to brush her cheek.

'Oh, my dear,' he whispered, his voice edged with mocking sympathy, 'if you tell him I'll sign his contracts, I think he'll agree to anything.'

Anything! Had he truly said anything? For a moment Ginny froze.

'You beast,' she choked out.

The silence between them was tangible, then he shrugged.

'That is hardly polite,' he said, his tone even, controlled, betraying not one atom of emotion. 'But what else do you expect me to think?'

His eyes locked deep into hers, dark, compelling, and he smiled again, but without the faintest trace of humour.

'So,' he continued, his words soft, smooth, remorseless, 'let us put it to the test, shall we? Tell him he can have the contracts, signatures and all, the day we leave Florence.'

What could she possibly say to that?

'Just as a companion? Nothing more?' she queried at last, her tone flat.

'Of course.'

'And there'd be no pressures, no trying to take it further?'

'You aren't still doubting my word?' he breathed, his voice hardening a fraction. 'I don't force my attentions on unwilling females.

56

Surely this evening has shown you that. You will come to me willingly, or not at all,' he added harshly.

'Then it's not at all,' she insisted. 'Do you give me your word on that?'

'I do,' he agreed.

'So we'll keep our distance at all times?' she persisted.

'Sweet Ginny, I never said that.'

Sharply, she looked up, her attention caught by his tone, and she quailed at the look on his dark face.

'I have never promised you that,' he said again. 'I want to show you what it's like to be loved by a man who finds you truly attractive. I intend to wine you, dine you, and win you. On that I also give you my word. You will come to me, one day. But it will be willingly, freely, of your own accord.'

'Never!' she exclaimed in a voice she hardly recognised as her own.

'Of your own accord,' he repeated.

Standing there, so tall, so sure, he appeared indomitable. He left her then, and taking his coat from the hallstand, he slipped it on and made for the door. Outside, the street was dark, empty, and the rain had increased to a steady downpour. The rush of cold air made her shiver, and Alex paused on the threshold, turning up his collar against the chill.

'I will call for you on Tuesday, on the way to the airport,' he said in matter-of-fact tones.

'Be ready, my dear. I don't like to be kept waiting.'

The door closed, sharply, cutting out the sight of him, and the apartment fell into silence again. For how long she stood there, unmoving, scarcely even daring to breathe, Ginny had no idea. Minutes maybe. She couldn't tell. But the need to sit down was overwhelming, and she fumbled her way into the bedroom. Slowly, she sank on to the bed. Her knees were trembling, her mind too dazed to function. What on earth was happening to her? Had Alex really kissed her like that, stirring her like no other man?

Restlessly, she rose to her feet again. Perhaps if she undressed, got ready for bed, this confusing see-saw of emotions would finally settle down. Sitting there thinking was only making things worse. The bedroom was warm, quiet, and she stripped off her finery and removed any faint traces of make-up still left on her face. Then she slipped into bed, burying her head into the freshly-laundered pillows.

Morning was almost breaking before she finally fell asleep.

Ginny might have slept for hours if the telephone hadn't rung so early. She started up, her eyes bemused by the sudden noise, but she'd guessed before she even picked up the receiver who it would be at the other end.

'Will?' she breathed, and she was right.

'Has Bergovich gone?' he demanded at once, his voice brusque.

'Of course he's gone. He went last night,' she retorted swiftly. 'What else did you expect?'

What was he suggesting? For once, she was in no mood to indulge him. Her eyes were heavy, and her head was aching from lack of sleep. What she needed now was comfort. Couldn't Will see that?

'I'm sorry,' Will murmured again, sounding instantly softer, sorrier. 'Did he try anything on?' he added, blurting out the things that obviously worried him most.

Ginny sighed, but she felt her irritation already starting to disappear. Poor Will. Of course he was anxious. Wouldn't she be anxious in his shoes?

'Nothing I couldn't handle,' she reassured him in soothing tones.

It wasn't quite true, but what else could she tell him over the phone? How could she explain the feelings Alex had aroused? Will would never understand. She didn't understand herself.

'Are you sure?' he began. 'Oh, Ginny, I've been so worried.'

'There's no need,' she insisted, 'really no need at all.'

Her voice sounded strained, exhausted, even to her own ears, and she stammered to a halt. But he accepted her reassurances without question.

'Good,' he breathed, 'but I'm coming over, right away. I can't wait to see you.'

Did he really have to do that, on the one morning she needed a couple of hours to herself? But she forced a false brightness into her voice when she answered.

'That would be lovely,' she responded, and maybe it would.

Maybe she was under-rating him. Maybe he wouldn't hear of her going to Florence, would put a stop to the whole stupid affair. Slowly, she put down the receiver and got out of bed. She took a shower, hoping the warm water would revive her. But, taking a swift look in the mirror, her heart sank. She still looked half-dead, her skin pallid, her eyes lifeless and heavy.

The dress from the evening before lay in shimmering splendour over the back of a chair, and she tucked it hastily into the wardrobe. A pair of casual trousers in cream linen were far more suitable for today, and she slipped them on, matching them with a longline tunic.

Will arrived within the hour, sweeping her into his arms the second he stepped through the door, pressing warm kisses on to her upturned mouth.

'Oh, my love,' he whispered, 'are you all right?'

'Of course I'm all right,' she assured him

softly.

But she wasn't all right. She felt awful; the whole situation felt awful. Breaking the news of Bergovich's plans didn't make her feel any better.

'What do you mean, as his companion?' Will queried, his eyes dark with questions, for which she had no ready answers.

'Only that,' she answered. 'All Alex wants is someone to keep him company while he's over in Florence.'

'So it's Alex now,' Will broke in harshly, his lips twisted.

Ginny bit her lip. He didn't understand. He wasn't even trying. Miserably, she lifted a hand, pushing a stray lock of hair from her face. Whatever she did, she was doing for him. Surely he could see that?

'We were at a party,' she reminded him quickly. 'What did you think I would call him? Sir?'

'I didn't think you would take him home.'

She hesitated at that, her features white, strained, and slowly, she nodded in agreement.

'You're right,' she conceded heavily. 'And I can't go with him. It wouldn't be right.'

Her head was bent, her tone low, but inside, her heart was singing like a lark. Will wouldn't let her go. There would be no conflict, no worrying feelings to rise up and torment her. She could stay at home, with him, and be safe.

'But I didn't say that,' he broke in,

shattering her new hopes.

Whitefaced, she searched his face for some sign of reassurance, but something seemed to be troubling him. He gazed down at his hands, fists clenched, his young features set and uneasy.

'Oh, Ginny,' he murmured at last, breaking into the uncomfortable silence, 'can I ask you something?'

Reality clutched like a fist at her heart, hard and cold as ice. She could guess what was coming next. He was again relying on her to find a way out.

'Alex will sign the contracts when we leave Florence,' she repeated, stating the words Will wanted to hear. 'He's given his word.'

Instantly, Will's face cleared, and he grabbed her into his arms.

'I knew you'd do it.' He laughed. 'I knew you'd find a way. Alex Bergovich is no match for you.'

Privately, Ginny had very definite doubts about that. Alex wasn't going to be any pushover, for her or anyone else.

'Let's hope so,' she said.

'You'll be fine,' he assured her.

Will took her out to lunch, telling her with a grin that she needed cheering up, and he treated her royally. He was so sweet, eager to please, that she felt herself smiling indulgently as he led her to her seat in the little wine bar he had chosen. It had always been a favourite of theirs, and after they'd eaten, they sat at their table in the window, sipping their tall glasses of chilled white wine. Gently, Ginny smiled at his lingering concerns.

'It shouldn't be too bad,' she assured him, forcing a note of calm and reason into her voice. 'It will only be for a week or two, and I can keep him at arm's length.'

'Are you sure about that?' Will queried.

Momentarily, it was her turn to drop her gaze. Was she kidding herself? Was she kidding Will? She hadn't told him everything, of Alex's promises, nor the strange magnetism he'd exerted over her own feelings. But, she reminded herself, nothing had happened. Gently, she smiled, taking Will's hand. Of course she could keep Alex at arm's length.

'I'm sure,' she stated firmly.

'What if he wants you to become involved with him?' he queried.

'Don't worry,' she put in, swiftly, sharply. 'Alex gave me his word—no personal feelings would enter into the arrangement. For some reason, all he wants is a female companion in Florence.'

'Just remember, he's no fool. He might try to pressurise you in exchange for the contract.'

Tenderly, she lifted a hand, smoothing away the furrows of doubt from between his eyes. Poor Will! How on earth could she blame him for leaning on her now? She'd never stopped him before.

'I'll remember,' she reassured him.

Tuesday dawned cold and clear, with an autumn sun struggling to shine in a pale blue sky. By mid-afternoon, Ginny was ready. Packing hadn't taken as long as she'd thought it would, and apart from seeing there was enough food in the kitchen cupboard to feed the cat, there wasn't much else to do. Her next-door neighbour had a key to come in and feed him.

The doorbell rang at precisely four o'clock, and Ginny almost leaped out of her skin at the strident tones in spite of the fact that she'd been expecting it at any minute. It had to be Alex. She lost no time flinging open the door, and there he was on the step, as large as life and looking as immaculate as ever. The faint, spicy scent of some very expensive cologne lingered on the air as he moved, filling her head with its sophisticated tang.

'Are you ready, my dear?' he enquired easily.

His strength was palpable, his dominance complete. Without a word, she nodded, and at a brief raise of his hand, the taxi driver came forward to take her cases. Automatically, she locked the flat. It would be days before she saw it again, days she scarcely dared think about.

'Come,' he said, holding out a hand. 'We have a plane to catch.'

CHAPTER FOUR

Twilight was gathering fast. Already lights were beginning to glow in the growing darkness. Bleakly, Ginny took the arm that was offered, allowing herself to be escorted out to the waiting cab. She was now alone with Aleksander Bergovich. She hadn't seen Will all day.

The flight was one of first-class attention. They wanted for nothing, and the luxury didn't stop there. A white stretch limousine was waiting for them at the airport, and they were whisked through the night to their hotel. Ginny wasn't surprised when the car drew to a halt in front of an ornate building in white and gold, its proportions almost palace-like in their splendour. She had known all along it would be the best.

The place loomed in sumptuous majesty overlooking the misty river, but she barely had time to take it all in before she was hurried through the darkened courtyard and into the glittering foyer. Once inside, Alex left her for a moment, to sign the register for them both.

He came back to her then, to take her arm, and together they followed the liveried porter escorting them to their rooms.

'The elevator,' the man informed them in almost faultless English, indicating the gilded gate of the nearest lift.

After seconds, the lift came down, whispering to rest in front of them. The gate slid open, revealing the imperious figure of a woman. Tall and elegantly dressed in designer white, with a pale, long-haired fur thrown about her shoulders, she had a groomed, sophisticated air about her. She swept past Ginny in a cloud of expensive perfume without even the cursory interest of a second glance. Suddenly, acutely, Ginny became aware of the business-like nature of her attire. Her suit was new, brand new, but its lines were dark and plain. It was obviously meant for the workplace, and in it, she stood out like a sore thumb in the midst of such luxurious surroundings.

'Shall we visit the boutiques in the morning?' Alex asked, a glimmer of amusement lightening his features.

She bit her lip in barely concealed irritation. Trust him not to miss the flash of dismay on her face, and then try to make something of it!

'Certainly not!' she snapped back.

He couldn't really imagine she cared what he thought? Briskly, she stepped into the lift, her features composed into a somewhat fixed smile.

'Come on,' she stated, putting on the least romantic voice she could muster. 'I'm dying to get my shoes off and have a cup of tea.'

If that didn't put him off any fancy ideas,

nothing would! He certainly didn't attempt another word as the lift glided silently upwards. They still didn't speak as they were shown into their suite, and once the luggage was stowed safely inside, Alex tipped the waiting porter. When he left, they were suddenly, completely, alone.

The atmosphere between them grew very slightly tense, but Ginny simply refused to panic. She would cope. Carefully avoiding his eyes, she strolled over towards the window, her manner determinedly calm. From where she stood she could see the river shimmering in the darkness, mysterious and romantic, the lights strung along its banks glowing in the evening mists.

'Florence is my favourite city,' Alex informed her with a smile. 'I shall enjoy showing it to you.'

'I shall enjoy seeing it,' Ginny breathed, and that, at least, was true.

'Do you want anything to eat?' he enquired politely, and at her hurried shake of the head, he shrugged his broad shoulders. 'Neither do I,' he agreed, 'but I will take a drink. Do you care to join me?'

She started to shake her head again, but he had already picked up the phone and was ordering champagne. Oh, well, she reflected resignedly, why not? After all, this is supposed to be a holiday. And when the bottle was brought in, resplendent in its silver cooler of ice, she managed two or three glasses. She even managed to enjoy them.

But it had been a long day, endless and strained, and it was now nearing midnight. If she didn't close her eyes soon, she would fall asleep on her feet. Carefully, she put down her glass.

'I think I'll go to bed,' she said, as casually as she could.

'Of course.'

He nodded, and his tone was so natural, so matter-of-fact, that Ginny positively heaved a sigh of relief. She rose to her feet.

'Tomorrow, I will take you to see the city from the Piazzale Michelangelo,' Alex promised. 'It's the only way to see Florence for the first time.'

'I'd love that.'

She smiled, pausing on her way to the door of her apartment.

'Good,' he said. 'It's a date, then.'

'It's a date,' she agreed.

She then showered, and slipped into her nightie before sliding thankfully beneath the welcoming quilt. The image of Will's face rose up under her closed eyelids, youthful, smiling, refusing to be denied, but she was alone now, in another country, a million light years away from him. Wearily, she buried her face in the pillow so that no-one would hear the faint, half-muffled sound of her tears. After a while, she fell asleep.

Ginny woke up with a jolt hours later. The curtains were drawn open, and daylight was streaming in through the windows. With a smothered groan of dismay, she sat bolt upright, suddenly realising it was morning. She'd hoped to be up, dressed, well before Alex appeared, but right on cue, he strode into her room, an easy smile on his dark face. She sank back against the pillows.

'Wake up, sleepy head,' he teased.

Carefully, she rolled on to her side, pretending sleep, but he made no attempt to approach her.

'Are you awake?' he enquired softly, and finally, she turned peeping, reluctant eyes his way.

To her surprise, she saw he was fully dressed, almost ready to go out.

'What's the time?' she yawned, doing her best to sound unconcerned.

'Breakfast time,' he said. 'I've ordered already, so it will be here any minute. You'll feel better after you've eaten.'

'I'd better get up.'

'No need.' He smiled. 'Rest. Eat it there. Then after breakfast, I thought you'd like to explore the old town.'

'Mm, yes,' she agreed.

'And if you like,' he added, 'we can have lunch at a little restaurant I know near the Ponte Vecchio. They make the most exquisite zabaglione you have ever tasted.'

69

'Show off,' she accused with mock severity, and when he threw back his head and laughed, humour glimmering in his eyes, she couldn't help but notice how different he looked— softer, more approachable, almost human.

It was mind-boggling to think that just over a month ago, he had been no more than a name to her. Before that, nothing at all. She had been going about her life, sublimely in love with Will, unaware of his very existence.

And now? She still knew nothing about him. She had no way of knowing.

A faint feather of unease shivered along her spine. The man was a mystery to her, a complete and utter unknown. He half-turned, seeing her eyes upon him, and he smiled. Quickly, she looked away. He was an attractive man, she had to admit it, but she didn't want to give him the wrong idea!

'Breakfast,' he said softly, as a knock came on the door.

They had a leisurely meal in the lounge of the suite, and afterwards he sat with his nose in the morning paper, giving her space to go off and shower and dress in peace. Fortunately, she'd thought to include some informal garments in her packing, and she slipped on narrow pants in wine-coloured silk teamed with a longline sweater in the softest ivory cashmere.

Later, they took a hired car, driving away from the town towards the soft, green hills of

Tuscany.

'Piazzale Michelangelo,' he said with a wave of his hand, finally pulling up in front of a broad, open square.

It was large, breezy, half-filled with dozens of market stalls, but he hurried her through the lot.

'There,' he said, and when she turned, she saw what he meant.

The view was incomparable. The square looked down over the full sweep of the city, to the cathedral's breathtaking cupola and beyond. Here and there, from the vista of white walls and roofs of burnished orange, rose Renaissance towers straight out of history.

'It's stunning,' she murmured, and he smiled.

'So I said,' he agreed, just a trifle smugly in her opinion.

He looked so inordinately pleased with himself, she chose to ignore him, leaning on the stone balustrade to get a better view. Under the slanting, autumn sunlight, the grey-green waters of the River Arno flowed through the very centre of the city, spanned by a host of slender bridges.

'There's the Ponte Vecchio,' Alex said as he leaned over her shoulder to point at a picturesque bridge in the distance. 'It has linked the two banks of the city for almost seven centuries. Think of the stories it could tell, of the Medici, Leonardo, Michelangelo himself, and Raphael, and we'll be able to see them all, or, at least, what they left behind them. And if you get bored with any of that ...'

'Bored!' she interjected, throwing him a raking look.

'Well, Florence is in the forefront of fashion these days, modern Italian fashion, that is, Armani and the like.'

'Ah,' she broke in, smiling.

'I thought that might interest you.'

They stayed on in Florence for two whole weeks, and apart from a couple of brief absences early on, Alex was always around. There seemed to be little business being done, and Ginny had the distinct feeling that the whole trip had been an excuse for his own selfish reasons. Not that it did him much good! She kept him strictly where he belonged, at arm's length.

But he proved to be a marvellous companion. He could make her laugh at the silliest things, and every day he found something new for her to marvel at. It was all so perfect, there were times when she realised she hadn't thought of Will for hours. When their last day dawned, they explored the shops in the city centre, a place of bright lights, plate glass, and arcades of designer boutiques. But window shopping was an idea Alex just didn't seem to be able to grasp. They hadn't come to stand outside on the pavement, he said in surprise.

Black leather sandals with slender heels, an Armani tunic, Florentine earrings worked in gold, were all bought and pressed upon her. No amount of protests cut any ice. In the end, Ginny kept silent. It was safer that way, unless she wanted the whole of Florence gift-wrapped to take home!

Afterwards, they sat in one of the open air cafés, sipping cups of coffee in the busy square. It was getting late. The sun was slipping away fast, the sky darkening to ebony velvet with a scatter of early stars. But the glittering lights of the city made the night more brilliant than the day.

'You have enjoyed Florence?' Alex enquired without looking up, his voice as polite as a stranger's.

'Oh, yes,' she murmured, and it was true.

It was a beautiful city, but tomorrow, they would be home. She would see Will, settle back into her old life again. Alex would soon be no more than a memory. Suddenly, there was a distinct chill in the air, and quickly, she drew her coat closer about her slender body.

'It's getting cold, we should go back to the hotel,' Alex insisted in concerned tones, his sharp eyes catching the faint shudder, and without waiting for an answer, he rose from his chair to help her to her feet.

'If you wish,' she agreed softly.

They dined at the hotel that evening, and Alex escorted her down to the restaurant, his guiding hand resting lightly on her shoulder. The dress she was wearing wasn't quite as revealing as the one she'd worn to the ball, and it was more classically cut. But it still left her shoulders virtually bare, and its clinging, dark pink lines fitted a lot more closely to her slender curves. In it, she graced his arm like a morning rose.

'You look quite lovely tonight,' he commented softly.

'Thank you, kind sir,' she returned demurely.

His compliments were always effusive, but she was almost used to them now, and she smiled, sweetly, keeping her voice light. The head waiter appeared at once. Alex didn't even need to lift his hand, and they were escorted swiftly to their table. Dozens of eyes followed their progress, female eyes for the most part. She could feel them boring into her back. Alex was the most flamboyant man in the room and certainly the most attractive, there was no denying that.

'I have something rather special for you,' he murmured as she slid gracefully into her seat.

Rather special was putting it mildly. With another of his gleaming smiles, he took a heart-shaped box in sumptuous dark red velvet from his inside jacket pocket, and he placed it on the snowy cloth in front of her. Carefully, he lifted the lid, revealing an elegant band of glittering sapphires and diamonds. Along its lower edge hung a row of perfect jewels, sapphire droplets gleaming like brilliants in the light. It was quite exquisite, and obviously very, very expensive.

'Alex,' she protested, her expression dismayed.

Oh, dear, she didn't want any more presents. He'd bought her enough already. But she could hardly say that, not here, with everyone watching.

'Ginny, my sweet,' he said, dark eyes hooded, intense, 'you surely aren't going to refuse it. It is a special occasion.'

'Special occasion?' she blurted out before she could stop herself.

'Our last evening here,' he said, reaching over to squeeze her hand.

Leaning forward, Alex smiled, his fingertips openly caressing hers.

'You must know my feelings,' he whispered, eyes alight.

'Maybe,' she breathed, 'but I didn't expect this.'

He rose, coming behind her chair to slip on the necklace. His fingers were warm on the nape of her neck, lingering against the sensitive skin just a little too long for her peace of mind.

'There,' he commented, 'it's quite perfect.'

The sighs in the room were almost audible.

The sparkling band encircled her throat as if it was made to lie there, its jewels glinting and gleaming in the candlelight, flashing blue fire. Serenely, Alex smiled down at her, satisfaction touching his mouth. But Ginny doggedly kept her eyes downcast, too stunned to smile back.

The meal was excellent and Alex was in a mind to linger over it, so it was past midnight before they finally rose from the table. Carefully, he took her wrap, slipping it about her shoulders.

'We must take care of you,' he murmured as he ushered her to the door.

'Mm,' she agreed.

She nodded, but her smile was distracted, her eyes distant. Her thoughts were drifting miles away, back home, back to her own world, the real world. Oh, she couldn't say she hated Alex any more, far from it. But, she insisted, he still wasn't Will.

One more night, just one night. Then she could go home. Wistfully, she lifted a slender hand to her throat, suddenly encountering the cold stones of the necklace under her fingertips. It felt heavy, its weight unfamiliar. Oh, why did he have to buy her something quite so precious? The man had been everything he said he would be, attentive, courteous, wining and dining her, but his behaviour could never be faulted. Suddenly, it was all too much. She needed a break, a breathing space, some time on her own to think.

'I'm just going along to the rest-room,' she said and excused herself.

She met Alex's eyes without flinching, and he nodded.

'I'll wait here,' he said.

'There's no need,' she put in quickly. 'I can find my own way back.'

'Don't be silly. I'll be at the bar. You won't be away for hours, will you?'

He was teasing her, she could hear it in his voice, and she shook her head, smiling back.

'Just a few minutes,' she promised, and with a tiny wave of the hand, she turned away.

When she reached the door, she glanced back, and he was still watching, still smiling, his dark brows raised. So she waved again, throwing him a serene, sideways smile, then she slipped quickly through the high, polished doorway. The rest-room was bright, lit with glittering artificial lights reflected off tall mirrors, cut glass, veined marble vanity tops. Ginny crossed to the nearest wash basin to rinse her hands.

Glancing into the mirror, she saw her own face gazing back at her, solemn-eyed, mouth straight and set. She twiddled at a stray curl, pulling it forwards over her ear, and overly conscious of Alex, waiting outside, she hurried, flicking her powder puff hastily over her face, patting out any hint of a shine from her pearly skin. A swift retouching of her lipstick followed, and she was ready to face him again.

Alex was in the bar, just as he said he would be. His tall figure was lounging at ease on one of the high stools, but a strange, hollow feeling stole over her when she saw he wasn't alone. Tall, red-haired, wearing a stunning creation in black velvet that clung to her every curve, a female figure was leaning across the bar towards him.

For a moment, Ginny froze. It was her! That woman. The model from the lift! She was ready to turn on her heel, leaving the wretched man to get on with his new conquest, but commonsense just stopped her in time. Why should she hide away like an unwanted intruder?

Carefully composing her face, she made her way across the crowded floor to approach the bar.

'Ah, Ginny,' Alex said and rose as she drew near, putting out a hand. 'Ginny is my companion,' he explained with a smile.

Companion? Is that how he described her? Ginny caught her breath, hating the cold knot of anguish suddenly gripping her. But she forced herself to meet his gaze, returning his smile with cool equanimity. Of course, she was his companion. What else would he call her?

'How sweet,' the woman purred, her smile just a shade too bright as eyes of the iciest blue roamed over the slender figure in front of her.

Sophia, as Ginny discovered she called

herself, made no secret of the fact that it was Alex she was interested in. Virtually turning her back on Ginny, she chatted away, her hands never still, carefully excluding anyone else from any real part in the conversation.

She was visiting Florence on a fashion shoot, so she said, which came as no surprise. She was so obviously a model. Her make-up was flawless, and in every way, she was the absolute picture of sophistication. The woman didn't possess an insecure bone in her body, Ginny reflected frostily. She was infinitely sure of herself, of her allure, certain that she could divert Alex's interest away from the naïve, young girl at his side.

'There's a small gathering in my suite later tonight,' the dreadful woman purred, 'for just a few select friends and acquaintances. A theatre director from Rome will be there, and a couple of designers from the local film industry. Would you and your friend care to join us?'

There was no mistaking the thread of malice in the soft voice, or the flicker of spiteful amusement in the brief glance she sent Ginny. Ginny returned the cold smile with dutiful politeness, but how would she cope if Alex said yes? Could she really spend the early hours of the morning, their last morning together, watching this woman make a play for him? Suddenly, Ginny saw red. Who did the woman think she was?

'I really don't know,' she broke in, the sweetest of smiles hovering about her lips. 'Alex and I have an early start in the morning.'

Alex and I? Had she really said that? Unexpectedly, she caught his eyes staring over at her, puzzlement in their dark depths, and a faint heat invaded her cheeks. Alex rose to his feet, an apology in his eyes. He took hold of Ginny's hand, threading his long fingers through her own, and, throwing Sophia one final smile, he began to move away.

'Ginny's right,' he drawled. 'We have an early start in the morning. Thank you anyway for the invitation.'

The woman's composure was admirable. Rejection must have been shattering to her ego, but her smile slipped for only a moment. Then she recovered at once. Throwing Alex a sultry glance, she shrugged.

'Some other time, maybe?'

'Maybe,' he returned, but there was no doubt his dismissal was final.

Ginny had no choice but to follow in his wake, but as soon as they were out of the woman's sight, she attempted to extricate herself. She was still seething inside. She was mad at Sophia, for just being Sophia! And mad at Alex for . . . for what?

Gritting her teeth, Ginny conceded she didn't know, but that didn't make her any less angry. She was mad at him, mad at herself!

'What on earth is the matter?' he hissed in

her ear. 'Surely you don't mind me speaking to Sophia?'

His eyes bore into hers, and a tinge of pink stained her cheeks. But her gaze rose to meet his, a defiant sparkle lending a brilliance to her eyes.

'It's of no interest to me whom you speak to,' she tossed back.

Alex looked down, his eyes darkly inscrutable, and her heart began to thud like a hammer. Surely she hadn't given him the wrong idea? He couldn't be imagining things, merely because she resented that wretched woman's haughty, high-handed ways?

'No?' he persisted with deadly softness.

'No,' Ginny returned quickly.

Alex said not a word, but his fingers tightened over hers, refusing to permit her escape.

'Let me go,' she hissed.

'Not until you can behave yourself,' he replied promptly.

'What?' she snapped. 'Me? Me, behave myself? Good grief, I'm not the one picking up strange women in bars.'

His brows shot up in mock disbelief.

'Unless you haven't noticed,' he broke in, his tone carefully even, 'the only strange woman I picked up in the bar this evening was you. I can't help it if other people speak to me, can I? Do you expect me to cut them dead?'

Ginny's chin lifted at a proud angle, but she

had to admit he was right.

'Maybe not,' she conceded softly.

For a moment he didn't speak, didn't react, his handsome features remaining quite impassive. Then slowly, he nodded.

'Very well,' he acknowledged at last, 'but just remember this, my sweet. I do not pick up women, strange or otherwise, especially when I am escorting someone else.'

'Just as you don't force yourself on unwilling females?' she enquired.

'Exactly so.'

With a quick smile, he bent his head towards her, and attempted to start moving along the corridor again.

'Ginny,' he implored under his breath, 'do you think we can go back to our room now? People are beginning to think I'm molesting you.'

'Rubbish.'

She grinned, but he was right.

He kept a warm hold on her hand all the way back, but, true to form, he let her go the moment they stepped into their suite. Unsmiling, he threw his jacket over a chair and pulled off his tie, his mind apparently elsewhere. Then he pressed a disc into the hi-fi, filling the room with sweet music.

'Drink?' he asked, opening the glass doors of the cabinet, and at the shake of her head, he shrugged, helping himself to a brandy.

He was as polite as ever. Sighing, she sank

down on to the settee, her feet curled up on the cushions. She was aching all over, but found herself strangely unwilling to go to bed. It wouldn't hurt to give him a few moments more, she thought to herself. After all, she would never have to see him again after tomorrow.

'Shall we dance?'

His voice broke suddenly into her thoughts, and startled, she glanced up. He was standing quite close, looking down at her with one hand extended.

'If you wish,' she murmured.

His clasp on her waist was light and warm as he gathered her to him. Dancing with him was always a pleasurable experience. He moved with surprising grace and rhythm, and they moved as one, bodies swaying together, lost in the haunting lilt of the melody.

'Again?' he queried as the music came to an end.

'Mm, yes,' she nodded, her eyes soft, half-closed.

But the next time was different. He gathered her into his arms and held her rather more closely. As he guided her round the floor, her steps faltered. Gradually, imperceptibly, all pretence at dancing ceased.

'Ginny,' he murmured, his voice no more than a whisper.

'No . . . no more,' she stammered, pulling away.

'Nervous of me?' he asked.

'Of course not!'

Uneasily, she moved away, towards the fireplace, not sure any more.

'Have you any idea,' he asked gently, 'how very lovely you are?'

'Alex, that's enough,' she warned. 'Remember your promise.'

'Which one?' he queried.

He had misunderstood her reaction to Sophia, her anger, the resentment she'd felt. He obviously thought the attraction between them was mutual, and now, she was having to face the consequences. Trembling a little, she took a deep breath to steady herself.

'You said you would keep your word,' she pointed out sharply. 'No involvement.'

'But I have, all this time,' he defended at once. 'Please, Ginny, don't you believe me? Didn't I say no strings? I would never make a play for you unless you felt the same way for me.'

His voice was so sure, so gentle, she paused, looking up. He was gazing down at her, his eyes more tender than she had ever seen them before. Swallowing nervously, she looked away, the strangest feeling fluttering along her spine. Suddenly, illogically, she wanted so much to believe him.

'Are you so afraid of me, little one?' he murmured.

'A little, maybe. I don't know,' she

stammered, not knowing what to say.

She couldn't think. Dazed, her eyes glanced away.

'But I would never hurt you.'

'Please, Alex,' she whispered, feeling totally lost.

Sighing, she looked his way, at his dark face, unsmiling at present, at the compelling eyes, sharp now with concern. It was true. She knew he would never hurt her.

He left her then, pausing for only a moment in the doorway, a long moment, to throw her an unsmiling look. His face was dark in the shadows.

'Trust me,' he repeated softly as he closed the door.

CHAPTER FIVE

Ginny woke with a start. The sun was streaming on to her face, telling her it was morning, and Alex was there, calling her name from the doorway.

'Ginny, it's time to get up,' he was repeating.

He was smiling, his eyes bright, but at once, she remembered his expression last night as he'd left her. Its image rose up before her, almost sad in the darkness, but there was no trace of sadness now.

'Come on,' he insisted. 'We're going home today. Remember?'

Home! How on earth could she have forgotten home? How could she have forgotten Will? She had to admit it. All she had thought of for days was Alex. Would she ever be able to look Will in the eyes again?

'Get up,' Alex's voice urged again, giving her no more time to think, 'or I'll have to come over there and help you personally.'

That threat concentrated her mind, sharply, instantly.

'You wouldn't dare,' she shot back, somewhat unwisely.

'Don't tempt me, my sweet,' he returned.

He often called her his sweet or his sweetness, and she thought she was used to it by now. But that morning, it caught her unaccountably on the quick, hurting unbearably. He shouldn't call her pet names, not if he didn't mean them. And she wasn't at all sure that he did.

'Ginny,' he countered, brow raised, 'what is the matter?'

She shrugged. That was the point. Perhaps nothing, perhaps everything. She simply couldn't tell.

'Nothing,' she forced out at last, not meeting his eyes.

'Then get up,' he insisted. 'Now!'

There was a thread of amusement in his voice, but he obviously had no intention of letting her lie in bed for another minute. He took a step into the room, and Ginny threw up her hands in consternation.

'All right, all right,' she cried out. 'I'm getting up.'

He was grinning as he left the room, acknowledging her surrender, setting her teeth sharply on edge. Balefully, she glowered over at him as he closed the door. The cheek of the man! Taking no chances, she sighed and got out of bed.

She went straight to the bathroom, and within minutes, she was up to her neck in warm, scented bubbles. The water felt wonderful, soft and soothing, and blissfully, she closed her eyes, sinking even further beneath the surface. But her thoughts were whirling almost out of control, pestering, tormenting.

What had she expected back there? A declaration of undying love? Abruptly, her mind stilled. Is that what she wanted from Alex?

Utter rubbish, she told herself sharply. Whatever next? Humming nonchalantly, she leaped out of the bath to wrap herself in a towel, and giving herself a brisk, all-over rub, she pushed the ludicrous idea right from her head. It wasn't even worth thinking about. Quickly, she slipped on her clothes for the day, a soft cream suit with a draped jacket and a straight, pencil slim skirt. It was teamed with a pale crêpe-de-chine blouse, and in it, she felt as elegant as any model.

Alex was still in his bedroom, and for once, she was the one who was dressed first. He'd left the door open.

'I won't be long,' he called. 'Breakfast will be here soon.'

Ginny sank into a chair. In a few hours, they would be going home, and she didn't know him any better than when they'd started out. Going home? Abruptly, she drew in a swift, uncomfortable breath, a terrible notion suddenly gripping her mind. Could that mean he was going back to Estonia?

Hadn't he said, oh, so often, how much she attracted him? But was it only a conquest he wanted, to gain control of her heart, her emotions? Would he leave her at the airport without even a second glance?

Sighing, she lifted a slender hand to her throat. Oh, however would she feel if he did something like that? In the silence, Ginny could hear him moving about, opening drawers, ruffling through the clothes in the wardrobe. A knock came at the door, and she heard the familiar sound of the breakfast trolley being wheeled across the carpeted floor. There was a brief murmur of voices, Alex's deep and easy, the maid's hurried and girlishly high. He was probably tipping her now, Ginny imagined, and generously, too, judging by the giggles of thanks. Then the door was closed, and it was quiet again.

He came back tall and confident, immaculately dressed in a white silk shirt and narrow, navy trousers. She didn't move as she watched him.

'Come,' he said, and when she didn't, added, 'Is something the matter?'

'Of course not,' she returned shortly.

He shook his head, his expression somewhat baffled.

'Then why so quiet?' he enquired.

Disappointment caught her a sharp jolt in the pit of her stomach. If he couldn't see for himself, if he wouldn't look beyond the end of his nose, there was nothing she could do to help him.

'Nothing.' She shrugged.

And what about you, she queried silently, her hands clenched at her sides. She dared a look into his face, trying to guess what he was thinking, but the handsome features didn't change.

'Now, shall we have breakfast?' he was saying.

So much for her hope of some hint of his feelings, however small. He took her arm, ushering her through his bedroom to the little sitting-room where breakfast was waiting. He was as attentive as ever over the meal, pouring her coffee, spreading her croissants with honey. His smile was assured across the table, his touch on her hand like silk. But she didn't eat as much usual. She finished her coffee, but she only nibbled at a croissant.

'You'll be hungry,' he warned. 'You've not had enough breakfast to keep a bird alive, and we won't be in London until well after lunch.'

So he was coming back to London, with her. Ginny tried to hide the wild rush of joy that she felt, dropping her eyes, toying again with her food.

'We?' she queried casually.

'I still have these contracts to sort out,' he returned with a shrug, 'and I want to make sure they reach the right place. He may be the love of your life, my dear, but I don't trust Shepherd an inch.'

The love of her life? Had he really said that? His voice stabbed like a knife, each word cutting her to the quick. Did he still think she felt the same about Will? Couldn't he see? These past weeks had been wonderful. He had made them wonderful. Nothing could ever be the same again.

Oh, no, she thought in a daze, does that mean I'm falling in love with Alex? The possibility left her stunned. Desperately, she tried to reject the idea. She was in love with Will. But she couldn't even conjure up the image of Will's face. It escaped her. All she could see was Alex.

'More coffee?' he enquired, lifting the pot towards her.

'No . . . no, thank you,' she stammered back.

Whatever happens, she thought with sudden certainty, Alex must never guess. This couldn't be love, not so soon. And what about Will, waiting so patiently for her to come home? She couldn't just walk away from him.

'Ready?' he asked as she forced down the last crumb, and at her nod, he helped her up from the table.

The journey back went without incident, but Ginny was dead tired by the time they got through customs, dead tired and heavy hearted, and she slept on and off for most of the time in the car.

'Home at last,' Alex said, gently touching her shoulder.

It was late afternoon on an overcast, wintry day and an early twilight was already beginning to fall.

'Where are we?' she stammered, peering into the gloom.

She hadn't a clue where they were. She was expecting to see her apartment building, but facing them was a tall, slender house at the end of an elegant terrace. Identical flights of white steps led up to a row of identical houses. There were white shutters at the windows, and white railings around the area steps. Only the doors were different. The one Alex was pointing at was painted cherry red.

'That's home.'

He smiled, obviously delighted by the bemused expression on her face.

'Home?' she echoed stupidly.

'Of course,' he replied, driving the car on to the short drive. 'A hotel suite is fine for an occasional visitor,' he added with a lift of his broad shoulders, 'but it is hardly suitable if I intend to be here on a regular basis. So I took a lease on this place. Come on,' he added, shrugging aside her surprise, 'we've wasted enough time. Let me show you around.'

Taking her arm, he escorted her to the front door, and, pushing it open, revealed an elegant, wood-panelled hallway. His footsteps were firm on the polished parquet floor as he led her into what was obviously the sitting-room. It was long and spacious, with high ceilings and windows overlooking an exclusive London square. At the far end, tall french doors opened on to a stone patio filled with plants and flower tubs.

'Do you like it?' he asked.

It was without doubt the most stylish room she had ever been in. Deep sofas and dark, polished tables were scattered over a carpet of delicate Chinese washed silk, and she was sure the paintings hung on the walls were originals.

'It's beautiful,' she murmured.

There was a fire blazing in the fireplace, a real fire with real logs, and with a quick smile, she crossed towards it.

'I thought you'd like that,' he said, his eyes fixed on her face.

He insisted on cooking her dinner, telling her she hadn't eaten properly all day, and she didn't argue. He surprised her by producing a very tasty vegetable pasta, done to a turn in a delicate herb sauce, with a perfect baked alaska to follow.

'Where did you learn to cook like this?' she asked in frank astonishment.

'There's a lot you don't know about me,' he reminded her.

'Then you'll have to tell me,' she prompted, 'I bet you were spoiled as a child,' she persisted, a brow lifted in his direction.

'When I was small, maybe,' he conceded slowly, 'but my family suffered much hardship as I grew older. I've had to work hard to get where I am.'

'Tell me,' she repeated softly.

'You may not like what you hear,' he warned.

'Maybe not,' she persisted, 'but I still want to know.'

She did, badly. She wanted to know him, wanted to know everything about him. Maybe it would help her to understand what was happening.

His face was sombre in the firelight, the strong features abruptly still. He was gazing into space, at some dim, faraway horizon only he could see. The teasing expression was quite gone.

'Most of my family are dead,' he began slowly, 'executed in prison or merely vanished. These things happened, all the time. The authorities didn't trust us, as we had connections in the West, and we were an important family in the old Estonia. So, we were constantly being harassed. Dissidents, I think they called us, but the name doesn't matter. The end was still the same. I lost my father, both my brothers, and the grief killed my mother.'

'You lost everything?' she queried, her voice low.

Such things didn't seem possible, not here, not in this warm, firelit room.

'I lost everything,' Alex confirmed, 'except myself. So I put myself to work. When Estonia became a free country again, I regained control of the family business. I worked all

94

hours of the day and night to bring it up to date. Oh, I was quite ruthless. I allowed for no opposition. It had to succeed. Now, it is the largest factory of its kind in Eastern Europe, and only one of the many business interests I have.'

Suddenly, Ginny felt incredibly small. Her life had been so safe, so comfortable and protected, compared with all Alex had been forced to suffer. Maybe he had made his work, his business, the centre of his life, but who on earth could blame him?

'Are you shocked?' he enquired, but she shook her head.

'Of course not,' she whispered, sympathy etched deep in her face.

She wanted to hug him, kiss him better, like a child.

'No wonder you want to leave,' she added quietly.

But she didn't get the chance to finish. His head shot up, the black eyes snapping denial, cold, instant denial.

'No, no,' he insisted, his tone appalled, 'you must never think that. I never would abandon my country. Estonia badly needs investment now, foreign investment, to get back on her feet. The best thing I can do for her is extend into the West. There are people back home, ordinary people, relying on me for jobs, for security, for a decent place to bring up their children. I have to think of them.'

He tossed out the facts, without expression, but Ginny could imagine the struggle, the denial, it had taken to keep things going. He was a formidable force, ruthless, single-minded, controlled. But not only to suit himself.

'I didn't realise . . .' she began, and his eyes softened.

Smiling, he shook his head.

'Why should you?' he murmured, lifting a long, lean finger to brush a stray curl away from her anxious face. 'You belong here, where no-one can hurt you, safe and warm in your own little world.'

'Alex,' she protested.

Her heart was aching with pain, with frustration. She didn't want to be safe in her own little world. He was her world now. Couldn't he see that? Wherever he was, no matter how hard it might be, she didn't care. Nothing else would do. The sound of a clock broke into the silence, whirring into life, chiming the hour, and she sat up to listen. It was already ten o'clock.

'I must go,' she stammered, rising to her feet.

There was no point in staying, not any longer, not tonight. He was never going to say the things she wanted to hear.

'But why?' he queried. 'I thought you'd be staying here.'

'Why should I want to stay here?' she

96

murmured, her voice scarcely more than a whisper, and he shrugged.

'Because I hoped we could stay together,' he said.

Pain gripped her heart, searing, alive, making her feel physically sick. She turned despairing eyes towards him, praying inside that she was mistaken. She had to be. He couldn't really be saying what she thought he was.

'I'd rather go to my flat,' she began.

'Nonsense,' he broke in.

Disbelief froze her rigid. Was this his love nest? Was he actually asking her to move in with him? She'd been tearing herself apart, wondering how he felt. Now she knew. He'd found them their own little love nest, in the best part of town, discreet and very expensive, where she would wait patiently for him to come and honour her with a visit.

'You belong in a house like this,' he insisted softly.

There, he'd finally put it in words. She belonged here, so he'd said, in his beautiful love nest, to be kept by him. Is that what he thought of her?

'No,' she repeated doggedly, 'I can't stay here.'

She couldn't. There was no pride, no dignity for her in this. But the words seemed to mean nothing to him. He leaned forward, an expression of genuine amusement glinting in his eyes. He threw her a sideways glance.

'We'll see,' he said.

He relaxed back against the cushions, an easy smile on his face, stretching his long body comfortably in the warmth of the fire. He looked so pleased with himself, she couldn't believe it. Resentment reared up inside her, resentment mixed with rage. What sort of woman did he think she was?

'How dare you?' she flung at him. 'I have never in my life come across such . . . such . . .'

She wanted to hurt him, wound him as he was wounding her, but she didn't know how.

'What on earth is the matter now?' he demanded, looking none too pleased at the outburst. 'You can't say you don't like the place.'

'Like it!' she flared. 'It doesn't matter if I like it. You should have asked me first!'

His eyes narrowed slightly and he shook his head.

'Ginny,' he said softly, 'what does it matter?'

'It matters to me,' she repeated harshly.

'But it would have spoiled the surprise,' he broke in.

'I can do without surprises like this!' she snapped back.

'Virginia Eve,' he blurted out, his hands raised, 'you are without doubt the most stubborn, the most awkward woman in the world.'

He obviously had no idea what he'd done.

No doubt, to him, women did as they were told, obeyed their menfolk. In Estonia, maybe, but this was London. He had to see things differently here.

'Oh, please accept my apologies,' she cut in, bitterness honing her voice to razor sharpness. 'Maybe the great Aleksander Bergovich is used to his women being more docile, more obedient.'

'Then he's come unstuck with you, hasn't he?'

The voice was barely a whisper, but she refused to feel intimidated.

'I'm not staying here,' she insisted.

'Why not?' he snapped. 'You still don't trust me, do you?'

'It's nothing to do with trust.'

'Of course it is,' he broke in. 'What else?'

What else? Ginny couldn't believe her ears.

'I'm old-fashioned, maybe,' she insisted, 'and perhaps you'll laugh. But to me, moving in here just wouldn't be right.'

Alex shook his head, his expression carved harshly in iron.

'Really?' he demanded. 'And why not? What's wrong with moving in with me, pray, now I've decided we should get married?'

CHAPTER SIX

Married? Had he really said married? For a second, shock struck Ginny utterly dumb, her breath caught in a tight knot in her throat. Her mouth opened, but no sounds came out, not even a squeak.

'Married?' she stammered finally.

He smiled then, nodding his head.

'Why not?' he shrugged. 'It's all worked perfectly well so far. We get on, don't we?' he persisted, conveniently forgetting the fact that they rarely saw eye to eye about anything!

'We do no such thing,' she protested, unable to be anything but hopelessly honest, even at a time like this.

'Ginny, we do,' he murmured. 'We could try harder. We could learn.'

'You mean me. I'd have to learn,' she countered dryly.

'To be a dutiful little wife,' he agreed, his tone silken smooth.

She almost said yes, there and then. She wanted to, so very much, and the word hovered irresistibly on the tip of her tongue. But just in time, commonsense prevailed, There was more to consider than her own feelings, no matter how vivid they seemed. So she shook her head, very slowly.

'This is very sudden,' she stated.

'Does it matter?' he queried.

Of course it didn't. It didn't matter at all. But she could hardly say that. She had to have time to think. There was so much to think about.

'May I have more time to consider?' she enquired.

'All the time in the world,' he agreed, 'as long as the answer is yes.'

'I can't promise anything,' she returned demurely.

Alex put a finger under her chin. Dark eyes searched deeply down into hers, compelling, holding her totally enthralled. Then gently, he tilted back her head until his lips could find hers.

'You will,' he promised huskily.

The kiss was infinitely sweet and tender, and he drew her into his arms. It felt so safe, so right, to be held there, as if nothing else in the world existed but them—Alex and Ginny, alone in their own special universe.

'No more, my love,' he whispered at last. 'There will be time enough, later on. This house is big enough for us to share. Stay independent if you wish, but at least give thought to my proposal.'

When Ginny woke the next morning, and, once dressed, went down for breakfast, she found Alex had already gone out. She sat deep in thought over a coffee. It was almost too much to believe, the changes that had overtaken her in just a few short days. Somewhere along the line, she knew, her feelings about Alex had undergone a total change. Now, she knew she was more than probably in love with him.

It was a sobering thought. But if she was being honest, maybe she'd always been a little in love with him and too afraid to admit it. Even at the start, when she'd been so sure she hated him, she'd tingled all over, whenever he'd been near. Just his presence had been enough.

And she needn't have gone to Florence. Oh, she might tell herself she did it for Will, for the contract, but deep down, she knew that simply wasn't completely true. She'd surely never been that gullible, that blindly enamoured of Will, that she would hand herself so completely over to Alex. Not unless some hidden part of her had secretly wanted to.

But was it love? To her it seemed real enough, but with Alex, there was a feeling of uncertainty, like riding a roller coaster that wasn't entirely under control. The familiarity, the safety, the little things that meant so much with Will, were all missing. Alex's thoughts on the rôle of women came straight out of the dark ages! Could she really hand her life over to him?

It wasn't as if he'd promised her anything in return. At least, none of the things she'd always thought mattered to her. Marriage, maybe, was on his agenda, but why? He'd never once mentioned love, even when he'd proposed. Shakily, she took a deep breath, unwelcome doubts rising up to torment her. Alex would have to love her, he would have to learn. There was no other way if she was going to consider his proposal seriously. The more she thought of how businesslike the affair was, the more angry she became.

Sunshine was streaming in through the French windows, and she squinted over at it. It was cold outside, but it was clear, bright, and she pushed open the tall, glass doors. Maybe some fresh air would help.

'There'll be room for dinner parties on the terrace in summer.'

Alex's deep voice broke into her thoughts, and Ginny was jerked back too quickly into the present. He was watching closely from the doorway.

'Mm,' she returned, with a faintly dismissive air.

'Yes,' he continued gravely, 'but for now, I think you should come inside. You're turning blue with cold out there.'

The wind was definitely chilly, and he was probably right. So she took the hand outstretched towards her, and allowed him to escort her in.

The next hour proved to be about the longest she'd ever had to live through. Utterly relaxed in his chair, Alex chatted as readily as ever, while all she wanted to do was escape. She couldn't indulge in small talk, not with her pain bubbling so close to the surface. Suddenly, she couldn't wait to be alone. He rose to his feet and strode across to the front door. She could hear his steps taking him purposefully across the polished hallway.

'Now,' he called back, 'I have a surprise for you. That's why I was out.'

'No, Alex, no,' she cried out. 'I don't want any more presents.'

'You'll want this one,' he insisted.

When he came back, he was clutching a wicker basket tentatively in front of him. From its interior came a whole crescendo of wailing.

'Thai,' she cried.

She would know the sound of her cat anywhere. In a trice, she opened the lid and lifted out the indignant Siamese. His protests diminished a little as she hugged him to her.

'I collected him this morning,' Alex explained. 'He's been alone long enough in that flat, wondering where you'd got to.'

She buried her face in the cat's soft fur. It was a small comfort, feeling Thai begin to soften against her, hearing the familiar purr start up in his throat. Alex came back to his seat.

'I shall be lunching out,' he informed her, 'with Thomas King, since I gave my word I'd finish the deal today.'

To her surprise, Ginny found she didn't

much care. Thomas King belonged to her other life, her previous life. She hadn't thought of him for ages, though it seemed the same couldn't be said of Alex. To him, business went on as usual. He cared so much for his work, his tenants, his employees. He would never knowingly let them down. But she needed him, too. Why couldn't he see that?

'So you'll be signing the contract today?' she queried.

At least, Will would be happy then.

'Of course,' he returned, 'and I must say, you did a good job, though it still grieves me to see Shepherd getting the credit.'

'It was his project,' she began.

Automatically, she defended Will. Somehow, she had to. She had betrayed him enough, without abandoning him altogether.

'It was your project,' Alex interrupted, his tone cutting. 'Do you think I hadn't worked that one out? You forget,' he added harshly, 'that I saw what he had to offer before you came on the scene, and it was far from impressive.'

'It might have been a little disorganised.'

'It was a mess,' he insisted, 'not worth a second glance. If it was left to me, the man wouldn't even keep his job.'

'Oh, Alex,' she broke in, shaking her head, 'Will might be inefficient, a bit inefficient,' she corrected guiltily, 'but he's not dishonest.'

'Not dishonest!' Alex exclaimed.

His face was thunderous, and she stared over at him, taken aback.

'What would you call what he did?' he demanded abruptly. 'Using his knowledge? Ginny, he was buying up shares at a low price, fully aware how much they would rise when this deal went through. Don't you see, he was using me, using my business, to line his own pockets.'

'Insider trading?' she gasped, unable to believe what she was hearing.

'Insider trading,' Alex affirmed, putting the final nail in the coffin.

Too shaken for words, she dropped Thai on to the carpet.

'Are you sure?' Ginny stuttered.

Would Will ever do such a thing? Use her, to back up a lie, to help him cheat in order to line his own pockets? It couldn't be possible. But a hundred little pieces fell abruptly into place—Will's desperation, his fear, his earlier hints at the good fortune to come. Suddenly, it all seemed to make a horrible kind of sense. Suddenly, she felt drained. No wonder Alex had been so odd with her at first. He must have thought she was part of the deal.

'I didn't know,' she informed him, her tone bleak.

'I gathered that, in the end,' he acknowledged, 'though for a time, I wondered, especially when Shepherd tried to use the promise of you, before the party, to get himself out of trouble.'

'No,' she flared, 'that isn't true. Will only needed me on his side, to help with the contract.'

'Really?'

Trembling, she shook her head. She couldn't believe this of Will. Hadn't he told her he loved her, over and over again? He would never exchange her for a contract. Alex must have misunderstood.

'I can't listen to this,' she stammered, moving blindly towards the door.

'So you believe in him still, the wretched Will Shepherd?' he demanded.

'But he is . . . was . . . my fiancé, my friend,' she tried to explain.

What Alex had said was harsh, hateful. She had known Will for so long, believed she had loved him. She wouldn't condemn him out of hand. But Alex's face was a picture, darkly incredulous.

'You are the most stubborn woman I have ever come across,' he snapped, 'and too independent for your own good.'

'Don't be ridiculous,' she broke in.

If this was what life would be like, married to him, there was no way she could do it. She could love him, be there for him, that part was easy, but she couldn't cope with his dictatorial ways. Rigidly, she composed her face, glaring down at her hands, clutched together in tight, little fists. It was time now to accept the truth.

She was wasting her time. Love couldn't be taught, in Alex or anyone else. It had to be there to start with.

'I'm a free person,' she continued stiffly, 'free to do as I please.'

'Not once we're married,' he threw back, with a shrug of those broad shoulders. 'I'll expect you to agree with me, support my wishes. You have a good head on your shoulders, you should be an asset to the business.'

Ginny took a deep breath, her eyes widening under his imperious gaze. So that was it. She was an asset to his business. She should have guessed that was all.

'How very interesting,' she retorted. 'And what exactly would be in this marriage for me?'

He indicated about the elegant room with an expansive hand.

'I thought it was obvious,' he returned. 'I can provide for you, give you every luxury you can imagine. Surely, we can agree terms.'

'Terms!' she gasped, shocked to the core. 'Not everything can be arranged like a business deal! No,' she insisted. 'No, no!'

He got to his feet, throwing her one long, last, disbelieving look, and she closed her eyes against his forceful gaze.

'I'll spend tonight at the hotel,' he began.

Ginny shrugged, meeting his gaze with icy eyes. She didn't care. She must have been mad to think for a moment they might have a future together. He was no different from Will, wanting her only for what she could do for him.

'Suit yourself,' she returned softly, and he turned on his heel and left.

The silence was suddenly overwhelming. What a miserable mess, she whispered. He'd lost his temper, she'd lost hers. They couldn't be alone for five minutes without rubbing each other up the wrong way. What kind of life could they ever hope for together?

'No life at all,' she acknowledged aloud.

Listlessly, she went to the window, watching him go. He glanced upwards, just once, but she stepped back behind the heavy velvet curtain, pretending she hadn't seen. When she looked out again, the car was already halfway along the road. For an age she stared sightlessly after it, torn apart by warring emotions. He didn't love her. That was more than evident. So why on earth did she suddenly feel so bereft? Surely, surely, she couldn't want him back, not after all he'd said.

Bleakly, she turned back into the room, but there was nothing to comfort her there. The fire was crackling just as merrily, the furnishings were just as luxurious, but it was all too quiet, too empty. She hated it now. She wandered through to the kitchen, restless and ill-at-ease. She switched on the kettle to make a drink, tears hovering horribly close. Why on earth had she had to go and complicate things? She, Ginny Eve, no less, the perfect secretary, the woman so much in control, had fallen head over heels in love, and with a man who couldn't care less.

'Damn you, Aleksander Bergovich!' she cursed shakily.

She reached for a mug, making the coffee hot and strong. She decided to drink it in the library.

The last of the winter sunshine was filtering in through the tall windows, throwing a pearly half-light on to the booklined shelves. Unsmiling she slid into a seat, curling her feet up beneath her as she sipped her coffee. She had to think. On one side there was Alex, hard, powerful, pulling her inexorably his way. Life with him would never be easy. But what about living without him? She took a deep, shuddering breath. She couldn't go back to Will as if nothing had happened, that was for sure.

An image of Will's face, smooth and untroubled, flashed suddenly into her mind, and her head drooped. She should go to him now, tell him, hear what he had to say. The telephone was in her hand almost before she knew it. She dialled quickly, before she could change her mind.

'Will Shepherd's office, can I help you?' a voice enquired in her ear.

'Yes,' she responded, trying to sound calm,

unconcerned. 'This is his secretary Ginny Eve. May I speak to Mr Shepherd?'

Secretary? Is that how she saw herself now, just his secretary? Uneasily, she twisted in her seat. Then abruptly, his voice was on the line, sounding so familiar, so unchanged, that an unconscious sigh slipped through her lips.

'Ginny,' he cried, 'this is a surprise. I didn't know you were back.'

There was no mistaking the delight in his voice. Instinctively she stiffened. She could hardly bring herself to reply.

'We . . . we . . . came back last night,' she stammered at last.

Her voice was unsure, stumbling over any reference to Alex. This was really hard, harder even than she'd imagined.

'I see,' Will began.

He didn't see, though. He couldn't see, not like this, not on the telephone. She took a deep breath.

'We need to meet, soon,' she stated, her tone suddenly firm.

'It sounds important,' he put in.

It was his turn to sound unsure, and instinctively, she took up the lead.

'It is,' she insisted, and he broke in before she could say any more.

'Come to the Champagne Cork,' he said, 'just after four.'

She dropped the phone back on its cradle, deliberately cutting the conversation short.

There was no point in going on, not until she was facing him, looking him in the eyes. She called a cab and got herself ready.

The cab came on time, and the traffic was easier than she expected. She was deposited outside their meeting place with fully five minutes to spare. Ginny pushed her way across the crowded pavement. The Champagne Cork had always been special to them, a place for shared laughter, for planning their future. They had celebrated their engagement in its romantic atmosphere. Now she had to sit there, tell him it was over between them. For what seemed an age, she stood in the doorway, staring up at its fancy sign flickering in the darkness. Her feet simply refused to take her inside.

'Ginny. Here, Ginny.'

Her attention was caught by the sound of a familiar voice, and she turned towards it. It was Will, of course, the same as ever, eager, boyish, smiling at her through the window. He had managed to secure their favourite table, and he was standing over it, beckoning to her. Nodding, she pushed her way through the door to pick her way towards him.

'Ginny,' Will called. 'It's so good to see you.'

His lips touched hers before she could stop him, not that she would have denied him a kiss. But then his arms drew her closer.

'It's good to see you, too,' she murmured.

But unobtrusively, she extricated herself.

'Sit down, sit down, let me look at you,' he was saying, ushering her quickly into her chair.

Thankfully, she sank down, but she couldn't look at him, couldn't meet those welcoming eyes. She removed her gloves, carefully, finger by finger.

'They are very nice,' he said with a wry smile, reaching out to take one from her nerveless hand. 'And very expensive, too, I shouldn't wonder.'

'Alex bought them for me, in Florence,' she intoned, doing her best to keep her voice neutral.

He threw her a sharp look, a sudden doubt in his eyes, and she pulled away, hastily dropping her gaze. Had he guessed already, that she was in love with Alex? A sudden shiver feathered along her spine. Was it written so clearly over her face?

'He was very generous,' she began, but she couldn't go on.

Abruptly, she broke off, hopelessly at a loss. To save her life, she couldn't have met his eyes.

The tension hung in the air between them, almost palpable in the suffocating silence. Ginny knew she was meant to leap in, reassure him, but her mouth was too dry. No sound would come. Silently, she raised her eyes. There was no going back, not now. Come what may, it was time to tell Will the truth.

CHAPTER SEVEN

Ginny could scarcely breathe. Her heart seemed to be turning painful somersaults in her breast, and in the tense silence, Will's eyes searched deep into hers.

'Ginny?' he stammered, his uncertainty very evident now.

There was no time for thinking, for searching for less hurtful ways to explain. It was too late for any of that. It was over between them, and she had to say so. Speechlessly, she stared back at him, her eyes wide. But she didn't need to say a word.

'Oh, no,' he groaned, his face ashen. 'I should have known. Bergovich is too full of himself, too determined, even for you.'

He stared down at the table, not meeting her eyes.

'But I made you go,' he continued, half to himself. 'This is all my doing.'

'No, Will, no,' she broke in. 'It wasn't like that,' she corrected quickly.

She couldn't let him go on blaming Alex or himself for what had happened. He glanced over at her, looking up at last, his eyes bemused, without understanding.

'Then what was it like?' he asked directly. 'How did he treat you?'

Sighing, she shook her head. It was

impossible to explain Alex to him; how much she loved him, yearned to be part of his life.

'He ... Alex ... wasn't what I expected.'

Carefully, she tried to put her feelings into words, but he broke in.

'Oh, no?' he queried harshly. 'So what was he? The perfect lover?'

She shook her head, lost entirely for words. Dumbly, she stared at him.

'Sir? Madam? Are you ready to order?'

The crisp voice of the waiter cut into the silence. Shakily, Will glanced up, trying hard to appear unconcerned.

'Half a bottle of the house white,' he stated.

'Of course, sir. It will be with you in a moment.'

The waiter was as good as his word. Within moments, the carafe of wine was placed on the table in front of them. Mechanically, Will went through the act of tasting and accepting it.

'Thank you,' he acknowledged, his smile fixed, and the waiter disappeared with a nod. 'Now,' he added to Ginny, filling her glass to the brim, 'what else have you got to tell me about Bergovich? What's going on between you?'

Ginny swallowed hard. The time had arrived for the truth, the entire truth.

'What do you want to know?' she breathed.

'I want to know what happened,' he demanded at once.

'Nothing happened, nothing at all like you

seem to think,' she insisted with a small, distracted sigh. 'Alex was the perfect gentleman at all times.'

The silence between them was leaden, stifling. Quickly, she glanced over at him, but any words she'd intended to say died at the sight of his face.

'Oh, Ginny,' he groaned, his eyes searching her downcast features. 'You've succumbed to him, haven't you? For me? For the contract? You did it for me.'

His voice was low, his eyes full of questions. It seemed he could think of nothing else. The colour drained from her face. Did he honestly think she was capable of such behaviour?

'It wasn't like that,' she returned hoarsely.

'Then what was it like?' he flashed back.

She shook her head, a hand reaching up to push the dark hair back from her face. She couldn't let this go on, for Alex's sake, and her own.

'He didn't touch me,' she insisted at last.

'I don't understand,' he muttered.

'Nothing happened between us,' she repeated.

If nothing else, she had to make him understand that.

'Oh, Ginny,' he whispered, 'don't lie to me. There's no need to deny it. I know you would only have done it for me.'

It wasn't true, but he wouldn't take 'no' for an answer. Hateful as it might be, hateful and infinitely sad, it was time for her to face facts. In spite of all his reassurances to her, his words of concerned warning, it was all a pretence. Will had deliberately sent her away to Florence, guessing the lengths she might have to go to to get a signature on his contract.

'It wasn't like that,' she began again.

Quickly, she tried to blink away the tears, but they formed again and again, quivering like crystals on her dark lashes. A brief smile curved his lips and gently, for the first time since they'd sat down, he reached out to touch her, lifting a hand to brush the shining drops away.

'Don't worry,' he whispered. 'It won't make any difference to me. I can live with this. We can live with it. We can put it behind us, work things out.'

'No, Will! No!' she broke in.

She had to make him stop, make him realise the truth. But it wasn't any good. If she'd had any doubts before, she certainly hadn't now.

'There's no future for us,' she insisted shakily, 'not any more.'

'Why not?' he insisted.

He sounded almost sulky, like a little boy denied his lollipop, and she watched him carefully from beneath her lower lashes.

'Think about it,' she whispered. 'We could never have been in love, not really in love.'

'Speak for yourself,' he hissed, whitefaced.

'It's true,' she persisted, 'or you'd never

have let me go with Alex in the first place.'

'So it's all my fault,' he replied quickly.

It probably was, the whole, sorry situation, but he would never admit it. His chin was raised, his features made small and mean with anger.

'I'm not trying to blame anyone,' she began, struggling to explain, 'but we have to be honest with each other. If you'd truly loved me, nothing, not even the contract, would have induced you to agree to my going away with another man.'

'You said you could take care of yourself.'

'You wouldn't have taken that chance.'

There was a short, tense silence, and Will avoided her eyes.

'I don't know,' he conceded reluctantly.

'You do,' she insisted. 'We both do.'

He still couldn't accept it. She could see it in his jutting lip, in the harsh set of his face.

'We needed that contract for us,' he stated flatly, 'so that we could get married.'

'No, Will,' she broke in. 'We needed the contract to get you out of trouble, and you were prepared to turn a blind eye to how I helped you.'

'You are blaming me,' he growled.

'No,' she corrected, 'I'm blaming no-one. I just want to understand.'

He smiled again, very gently, and he reached over to entwine her slender fingers between his own.

118

'But I do understand,' he assured her, 'and it doesn't matter. Nothing matters but us, our future. It could be wonderful now. Thomas King can't do enough for me after this.'

It was the wrong answer. She closed her eyes, the ache in her throat fast becoming unbearable. Once, she had almost hoped for this moment, the chance to return to all she'd known before Alex, a return to normality. But now, she could see there was no going back. Will wasn't the man for her. He had used her.

'It isn't any good,' she whispered, shaking her head.

A travesty of a smile twisted his lips and he stared hard into her face.

'But we love each other,' he insisted.

Again, Ginny shook her head, her eyes downcast. She couldn't pretend any longer.

'I thought we did,' she conceded, 'but now I know differently. Now I know what love really is. If you'd loved me, as much as I thought you did, you would never have sent me away with Alex regardless of his motives, which, by the way, weren't what you think. Loving is putting the other person first, putting their feelings, their happiness, before your own.'

'But we're good together,' he cut in.

'No,' she sighed, 'it was good only for you.'

What she had felt for him had been first love, young love, sweet and genuine in its way, but never likely to last. As for him, she wasn't sure any more which he'd valued most, herself, or what she could do for him.

'I'm sorry, Will,' she added, slowly, softly, 'but I've fallen in love, with someone else.'

'Not Bergovich?' he finished for her.

'Yes,' she acknowledged, her voice little more than a sigh.

It was the hardest word she'd ever had to utter, putting Will fully in the picture, but bravely she forced it out. Will took a deep, ragged breath, almost gasping for air, and her eyes flew to his face.

'But does the wretch love you?' he cried.

His tone was discernibly less warm. Already, there was a tinge of accusation in its depths. Her lips tightened, despair constricting her throat. She opened her mouth, trying to speak, only to close it again without uttering a word. He was right. Alex had never said that he loved her.

'No,' she managed at last.

For a moment he hesitated, not going on, as if he was struggling to find the right words.

'But I loved you,' he said eventually, shaking his head, 'and I thought you loved me.'

'Enough to allow me to go off with somebody else, to save you?'

The words were out before she could stop them, hanging like fire in the air between them. But Ginny didn't turn away, or lower her eyes. She had to find out, once and for all. For a moment, he didn't respond. He stared hard at her set features, his face carved in stone, then he finally shrugged.

'I might have thought of it like that,' he admitted bleakly.

'And mentioned the possibility to Alex?' she queried. 'Tempted him with the idea of having me as a companion?'

He didn't answer. He didn't have to. So he had suggested it, set it up, only Alex hadn't gone along with it in quite the way Will had thought he would, by taking advantage of her.

'Why not think you would go for him?' he said at last. 'Bergovich is a good-looking guy, and fairly experienced with women, I'd say.'

'Love means more than unfaithfulness to me,' she gasped.

'Does it?' he spat out. 'I wouldn't know. But it would have been proof, wouldn't it, that you loved me? That you would do anything for me? Instead, you've thrown it all away.'

He shrugged, avoiding her eyes, but his meaning was abundantly clear. It couldn't have been any clearer.

'Oh, yes,' she said angrily, her voice scarcely audible. 'You would have accepted anything as long as it was to help you out. But he was sweet, kind, caring, a gentleman, and I've fallen in love with him.'

His gaze remained steadfastly fixed on the table in front of him, and he didn't speak, didn't make any attempt to deny her words. Looking over at him, at his surly expression, at the compressed line of his mouth, she knew. It was true, all true. He didn't need to utter a sound.

'This wasn't how it was supposed to happen,' he muttered at last.

'But it has,' she murmured, finality edging into her voice.

Steadfastly, she met his eyes, and with a composed face, she rose to her feet. There was no future here. She had trusted him, believed him, and in return he had used her. He would still use her, given the chance. She shook her head. His ideas about the meaning of love were miles from her own.

Somehow, she got to the door. She glanced back, just once, catching only a blurred glimpse of Will's pale features before she found herself outside. Blindly, she raised her arm, and a taxi drew up at the kerb. Within minutes, it had whisked her away.

The drive back to the house seemed to take for ever. She couldn't think, couldn't feel, hardly dared breathe, and when the elegant terrace finally came into view, she was still feeling rather more than a little shaky. She would have preferred to go back to her flat, to leave them both behind her, Alex and Will. But there was Thai, waiting for her at the house. She had to collect him. Quickly, she climbed out of the cab, thrusting a handful of coins at the driver. Without waiting for any change, she left him muttering his thanks and went inside.

She made straight for the downstairs cloakroom. The room smelled faintly of flowers, but with a blinding headache coming on, she found the scent cloying, vaguely nauseating. Immediately, she snapped on the light, and she winced. Even the muted glow from above the vanity unit brought a stab of pain to her eyes. Fumbling towards the glass-fronted cabinet, she found a bottle of painkillers and dropped two of them into her hand. Perhaps, she sighed as she swallowed them hastily with some water, they would stop her headache before it got any worse.

Thankfully, there was no light on in the sitting-room, and Ginny didn't put her hand on the switch. Quietly, she sank into a chair, preferring the firelight throwing its burnished reflections into the shadows, illuminating the soft cream walls and the furniture's darkly polished surfaces with a rosy glow. She was tired, so tired her eyes could scarcely focus, but she couldn't face going to bed. So she made up the fire until the flames were roaring in the hearth, then she collapsed wearily into a chair.

Thai had stirred at the sudden activity, opening his disapproving eyes a fraction, then he leaped up on to her lap. Yawning, he curled against her, settling again, and she half-smiled at his obvious satisfaction. Slowly, she stroked his sleek body, her eyes misty with unshed tears. If only her own life was as simple as his!

123

She didn't even know anymore where it was heading. Love like hers, kept hidden, unrequited, led to nowhere but pain. But she couldn't go back to her old life, either. That was finished for good. She closed her eyes, sighing, shutting out the sight of the leaping flames. Whatever she did now, she had to do it alone.

Morning came at last, with the dawn of a cold, grey day. Ginny jumped up as the first streaks of daylight filtered in through the window, tipping an indignant Thai on to the carpet.

Gazing into the bathroom mirror, she saw an overly-pale reflection staring back at her, its eyes shadowed and listless from lack of sleep. Quickly, she washed the worst ravages of the night away, disguising them with skilful touches of make-up, and a deft flick of a comb through her tumbled hair brought the dark tresses under control.

Thankfully, Alex hadn't returned. She needed to get away before he put in an appearance. The thought of him coming back, of having to run the gauntlet of that dark, compelling smile, turned her bones to water. But Thai was pestering for his breakfast. He followed her into the kitchen, miaowing and weaving around her legs until she couldn't ignore him any longer. She finally gave in, filling his dish with as good a grace as she could muster. She watched as he settled over it with an approving purr, envying him his appetite. She couldn't have forced down a bite.

'Do hurry up,' she urged, but he wasn't in any rush to leave.

'Well, hard luck, we're going,' she muttered. 'You wouldn't have me stay where I wasn't wanted, would you?'

The poor animal had barely finished his last mouthful when she snatched him up and made for the door. It was time to go, but the wretched cat basket was nowhere to be seen. She fumed silently. Why do things have to go missing when you need them most? Finally, she located the wretched thing half-hidden behind a chair, but by then she was muttering like a madman and Thai had definitely had enough. Wriggling furiously, he loosened her grip and with one wild leap, he shot to the doorway, just as the door opened.

'What on earth!' a voice exclaimed as the cat leaped past into the hall.

'Alex?' she gasped.

Unobserved, he had let himself in, his arrival missed in her struggles with the cat. She bit her lip. It simply wasn't fair. No man had the right to look so good first thing in the morning, so handsome and self-assured.

'Ginny,' he returned, surprise raising his tone.

Confused, she gritted her teeth, mortification burning into her skin like fire. Did he have to come in now and catch her chasing the cat, out of breath and furious, with her hair all over her face?

'Well, you don't expect me to leave Thai behind, do you?' she demanded sharply.

'Behind?' he queried.

Balefully, she glared over at him, her eyes alight with determination. She wouldn't back down now.

'When I go, of course,' she flashed back.

She was rewarded by his instant, unfailing attention. There was an immediate silence, harsh and intense, and he came stalking into the room. If she'd announced she was emigrating, he couldn't have looked more appalled.

'Go?' he hissed. 'Go? But I haven't said you can go anywhere.'

Colour flared into her face under his narrowed gaze, then drained to leave her features paper-white. Suddenly, she was calm, icy calm. She knew what she had to do.

'I don't need your permission,' she interrupted with frigid finality, but his hand shot out, catching her arm.

'Listen to me,' he insisted, but she was way past heeding.

'You've said enough,' she informed him. 'Now let me go.'

'Not until you've heard what I have to say.'

His voice was flat, and she suddenly ceased to argue. It was too undignified, and besides, she knew there was no point when he used that tone. He would never give way.

'Very well,' she returned, conceding with a lift of her chin, 'but don't be long. I have things to do.'

Without further protest, she allowed him to guide her back to the sofa, and together they sat down.

'Well?' she demanded.

'I thought we were getting married,' he stated flatly.

'Yes,' she flung back, 'you thought so. I don't remember saying yes.'

But he evidently didn't think there was a problem, judging by the look of disbelief on his face.

'But you will,' he said, almost smiling.

He sounded so sure of himself, certain all he had to do was smile, turn on the charm, and she would fall at his feet. Well, he could think again. Carefully, she glanced upward, looking directly into his face.

'I'm very flattered,' she said, 'and I'm sure it's a wonderful offer, but I really must decline.'

She almost couldn't say it, not turn him down flat. But somehow, the words were forced out through stiffened lips. It was all she wanted, to marry Alex, to live as his wife, but not like this, with love only on her side. What hope was there in that?

His voice cut into her thoughts, sharply, a note of contempt edging into its deep tones.

'Now I understand,' he snapped. 'What a

fool I've been. It's Shepherd, isn't it? I've signed his contracts, so I've served my purpose. Now you're free to go back to him.'

She could scarcely believe it. Was he still going on about Will? What on earth was the matter with the man? Impatiently, she shook her head.

'This is nothing to do with Will,' she began frostily.

'I should hope not,' Alex ground out. 'Oh, Ginny,' he enquired with biting harshness, 'do you really still harbour the notion that Shepherd, that devious, dishonest youth, is the man for you? I've tried so hard, tried to show you what I could offer, yet you still hanker after him.'

He was being at his worst, autocratic, overbearing, on his high horse. But for once, the words went straight over her head. A small, nagging suspicion was taking form in her mind, a wild, improbable notion that made her head whirl just to think about it.

'He knew, you know, that I wanted you,' Alex snarled again. 'Right at the beginning I told him. I said you were too good for him, but he boasted that I could never take you away from him, and he was right.'

'What?' Ginny exclaimed.

He was right about Will, that was for certain. Devious was just the right word. Trading her for his contract hadn't been enough. He'd lied about Alex's intentions as

128

well, poisoning her mind, just to keep her tied to him. Apparently she was too useful to lose! No wonder he'd found it so hard to believe the truth about Alex. His ego must have been hurting so much. But that didn't matter now. Nothing mattered but Alex, standing over her with embittered eyes, his expression like ice.

'You're jealous,' she ventured. 'I do believe you're jealous of Will.'

'Don't be ridiculous,' he flashed back.

But Ginny shook her head, the penny finally dropping into place. She was right. Poor, weak, incompetent Will was the key to all this.

'Yes,' she persisted, 'you're jealous. You were jealous of Will all the time in Florence, you were jealous of him yesterday, and now, you're more jealous of him than ever, because you think I still want him.'

It all suddenly made sense, the inexplicable anger, the punctured male pride, the possessiveness, and she threw him an incredulous look. He was jealous of Will and her.

'It's true, isn't it?' she breathed.

Instantly, he stood up, a frown deepening between his dark brows.

'I don't know what you mean,' he insisted.

'You know exactly what I mean.'

There was another silence, but Ginny ignored his set expression, the imperious stare. They meant nothing now.

'You love me,' she whispered, 'don't you,

129

Alex?'

This time she held her breath, scarcely daring to hear his reply. Her very life hung on what he had to say. He drew himself up to his full height, his features carved in ice.

'What if you dislike the way I treat you, making you submit to being an obedient wife?'

'You won't!' she countered, suddenly fired with the conviction he loved her, in spite of himself.

'Maybe not,' he conceded, shrugging, 'but I need to live in Estonia for months on end.'

'Then I'll come with you,' Ginny retorted at once. 'I've always wanted to travel.'

A faint smile touched his lips, lightening his expression, and he sighed, deeply, shaking his head in mock despair.

'I can see you'll never make me a dutiful, Estonian wife,' he said softly.

'No,' she returned sweetly, 'but think of the fun you'll get from trying.'

He laughed at that, throwing back his dark head, genuine amusement lighting up those intent black eyes. He looked so much like the old Alex, her Alex, that her heart turned a whole series of somersaults.

'Oh, Ginny, Ginny,' he sighed, 'what am I going to do with you?'

'Love me,' she answered simply. 'Just say you love me.'

He turned agonised features towards her, his eyes filled with so many demons that a chill settled like ice in her bones.

'I can't,' he cried out.

Can't! The word was torn from him, exploding like a thunderbolt in the sudden silence, and she swallowed convulsively. What on earth did he mean?

'Can't?' she echoed fearfully.

'I can offer you marriage, security, everything you want,' he reiterated, his voice broken, lost, 'but not love. Please, don't ask for love.'

Her heart almost stopped beating, and she had to force herself to keep breathing.

'Why not?' she gasped. 'Why can't you love me?'

For a time, he wouldn't look her way. Then he raised dull, despairing eyes towards her.

'Oh, Ginny,' he broke in, 'don't you see? Everyone I love, I lose, one by one. I see them suffer, disappear, die. How could I ever do that to you?'

So there it was. Some unspeakable memory from his youth haunted him still, making him hide his feelings behind anger, behind a mask of haughty control, too afraid to ever risk loving again. What pain had he faced, to bring him to this? A former love, no doubt, snatched away without warning. Had he seen her die, powerless to help, like everyone else in his life? One day, when they knew each other so well that nothing else mattered, she would ask him again, hear the full story, but for now, he'd said enough.

'Oh, my love,' she said, 'things are different now. If I can take a chance on falling in love, surely you can, too?'

There was a moment of silence. Then Ginny did the one thing she wanted to do more than anything else in the world. Very slowly and carefully, she took Alex's face between her two palms, and she kissed him. For a split second, he didn't respond. Then his arms went about her, crushing her close, and he began to kiss her back. His lips found her mouth, deeply, possessively, claiming her utterly as his own.

'I do love you,' he whispered, 'I do,' and there was no hesitation, no mistaking his passion. 'Oh, Ginny, my Ginny, I think I've loved you right from the first.'

She smiled then, her eyes glowing. He loved her, he'd said so, and he thought he had from the first.

'Don't you know?' she queried.

'I didn't want to know,' he conceded slowly, sadly. 'I didn't want to admit it, even to myself. I didn't dare.'

'And now?'

'Now,' he whispered, 'I can't help myself. I couldn't do what Shepherd suggested, just take you, much as I wanted to. But I couldn't let you go, either. I had to keep you with me somehow.'

Slowly, she lifted a hand, sliding a tentative

finger across his mouth.

'So you offered me a business deal,' she teased gently, and he shrugged, miserably avoiding her eyes.

'It's all I know about, business deals,' he replied, his handsome features downcast. 'I didn't dare hope for more than that.'

He still wouldn't look her way. Her Alex, her wonderful Alex, so commanding, so much in control, was actually lost for words.

'Wasn't it obvious how much I was growing to love you?' she asked.

Her voice trembled to a halt, and she dropped her eyes, warm colour rising to tinge her soft skin with a rosy glow.

'Of course,' he admitted softly, taking her tenderly into his arms. 'For me, too, it was special, very special. That is what frightened me so much.'

'No more,' she broke in. 'No more talk of fear. From now on, we only talk of love.'

For a very long time he held her, his lips caressing her mouth, her throat.

'Enough, my love,' he murmured at last. 'We have a wedding to plan, and I can't wait.'

'No?' she asked, looking up.

'No,' he insisted, his face carefully solemn, 'and I have a special licence to prove it.'

'In case I run away to Will?' she queried gently.

Alex laughed, a sensual sound from deep in his throat, and he looked down at her upturned features, a fire in his dark eyes.

'Over my dead body,' he said.

Tenderly, Ginny smiled, turning shining eyes up towards him.

'Oh, Alex, Alex,' she sighed, 'all I want is to be with you, always, sharing your life, having your children.'

'Children.'

He drew back, his face a picture.

'I want lots of them, at least three or four. Do you think you can manage that?' she teased.

'You cheeky young madam!'

Ginny grinned, broadly, burying her face in the welcoming warmth of his shoulder. Marriage to Alex would certainly never be boring. Their skirmishes might be many and varied, but they would never be dull.

'I suppose,' he said and groaned, not missing that victorious, little grin and raising dark eyes despairingly to heaven, 'that I've just given in to all your demands.'

'Every last one,' she returned serenely. 'We belong together, Aleksander Bergovich, now and for ever, and don't you ever forget it.'

He threw her a slanting look, his eyes alight, and he enfolded her very closely in his arms.

'Oh, my own, sweet Ginny,' he whispered. 'You must remind me of that every day, for the rest of my life.'

'Of course,' she said softly, her smile promising him the earth.

We hope you have enjoyed this Large Print book. Other Chivers Press or G.K. Hall & Co. Large Print books are available at your library or directly from the publishers.

For more information about current and forthcoming titles, please call or write, without obligation, to:

Chivers Press Limited
Windsor Bridge Road
Bath BA2 3AX
England
Tel. (01225) 335336

OR

G.K. Hall & Co.
P.O. Box 159
Thorndike, Maine 04986
USA
Tel. (800) 223-2336

All our Large Print titles are designed for easy reading, and all our books are made to last.